CHASING DRAGONS

Copyright 2011 Thea Atkinsoon

Published by Thea Atkinson

Cover design by Thea Atkinson

Many thanks to some great beta readers who helped me improve the tale:
Richard Lewis, Brittany Atkinson, Jim Fay

ISBN 978-0-9921489-0-4

I0628304

Chapter 1

Sometimes I think about angels, and I'm not talking about those man-made, Plaster of Paris knockoffs either. You know that kind: chubby little bastards blowing kisses from dainty palms, their equally chubby little wings spread wide as a hooker's legs, a vapid smile curving their mouths. Nope. I don't like to think about those kind too much. Too many of them around my parents' house, you see; so many that I tell people they're what drove me to the evils of the big city four years ago.

What I do think about are the real ones: the seraphim, the guardian angels, the archangels. Those who fell from Heaven when they followed that most beautiful creature of all, as well as those who remained behind, stuck in paradise because they couldn't manage out-of-the box thinking. Those ones who, all, have smooth expanses of desert where there should be moist oases of genitals. Those beings created for servitude to the glory of God. Ah, no use for genitalia to do what they do; no, indeedy not. And as you know, genitalia is a very big part of life. It rules us by its very nature of flesh and folds.

Still, do angels think about what their existence would be like with genitals: with a clitoris to raise shudders on nerve endings from sole to soul or a sensitive tip to plunge into secret areas and buckle a sac deep into its surrounding body?

It makes me wonder if God in one of his exploratory moods granted Lucifer one of these accoutrements--or both, even--as an experiment, and ended up giving the creature an understanding of joining that the rest could never imagine.

Is that why they threw theology's greatest hissy fit?

It might reassure you to know that I do think of other things. I'm just like you; like most folks. I think about the economy and world peace. There's also the fact that a half-breed is the newest American President, happier to identify with his African side than his Caucasian for now because it ushers in 'a new era.' Not that I'm against all that. I think it's long overdue that a man of African descent could be President. An African American woman? Getting there. Better yet, what about a bi-racial, bisexual, cross dresser for president. We'd be making real strides as human beings then, now wouldn't we?

It matters to me, you see, that you understand just how like you I am. That I'm really a regular everyday kind of Joe. Or Josephine. Like you I worry about money, about work, about family. See? All very normal for a middle class heterosexual person.

Well, there is the tiny, very tiny, issue of what gender I am, and whether that gender is the same today as it was yesterday, but that's no big deal. Not really. Not when you remember how much crap is out there in the world to deal with. A little thing like gender relapse is so little to contend with after all.

But still, you want to know and I don't blame you. Be you woman or be you man, you ask. It's not a simple answer, to tell you the truth, and that puts me on the far left side of an already leftist rationale.

Let's just say that for the last six months I've been back in my small hometown, I've scraped a razor over my jaw every morning and spared my legs the razor. On Friday nights, I throw cologne beneath my armpits then onto my neck and I go out on the town to get laid, which here in rural Nova Scotia, means a thirty minute walk from my crappy little apartment in the south end to the only bar we have.

It has a patina on the outside that makes it look like

whiskey has seeped through the boards and enough dank on the inside that you can smell the chlamydia on every surface. No new efforts have gone into keeping the place clean, no new layer of varnish on the heel-gouged dance floor. No matter which restroom a body goes into, the toilets and urinals have deep tar colored stains that leak stench into the floors and walls. You feel dirty just looking at the sinks.

The place draws crowds like meth addicts to pharmacy brand cough syrup.

Last time I'd been out, about a month earlier, I'd gone home with a young lady who sported braces and looked like she needed a nipple for the beer bottle she was chugging from. Class act up the wazoo, sure as shooting, and just what I needed at the time because I'd been kept awake by the baby next door for more hours than I wanted to count.

Funny, when I moved in, I'd not thought about the consequences I'd have to endure living next to the very pregnant woman I'd glimpsed off and on at the mailbox. That the belly she sported would erupt in an invisible mass of unending cries so shrill they sent the little bones in my ears into spasms.

So I had a lot of frustration to release. Luckily, braces girl was into that. But like I said, that was a month past and I was getting about ready for another kick at the can. So when Molly messaged me that she was coming home for the weekend and that she could manage a trip 'down the Bay' as she called it so we could party together. I messaged back that we should make plenty of time to catch up before the place filled with loud drunks--say before the small hand could jerk its way to 10 pm. She would like that phraseology, Molly would. Her nature was, how shall I say, tremendously sexist. I could imagine her grinning at the message, and indeed when I got back, a stuck out tongue smiley, I knew she was lolling her own at the screen as she did so.

She was a pretty literal gal for a lesbian -- a product of her nurture rather than nature. She had been brought up in

Clare--a mere half hour from me--in a village so Catholic and so old fashioned that they still named a good deal of their kids after saints.

It was a pity that, though we'd lived so close all our lives, Molly and I had not found each other before we each moved out, separately, to the big city three hours away, where both of us ended up binging on queer mixers and gay bars the way dieters do on chocolate.

I knew, by the way she'd be partying once she got home, that she'd not want to stay at my place. My five-room apartment had obviously been a larger house at one time, and the landlord had broken it into three apartments so he could triple his income. I slept too close to that girl and her squalling baby and had to mention it to Molly; you know, just in case.

"No fucken way," she'd written and I imagined her saying it, the way she had of talking that made curses sound like she was chewing on a fat wad of pink bubblegum.

In the end, we both agreed a hotel room would be way cheaper on her pocket than a cab ride all the way back the thirty minutes to Clare and easier on both our hung over nerves than having to jumble out of bed at five am, thinking by the squalls we had to prep formula.

Decision made, I rumbled from my house via cab on into the parking lot of the bar. There was a cluster of young men hanging outside. The smell of skunk permeated the air and wafted off their clothes as I drew close: weed. I couldn't help a snuff of user-snobbery as I walked by. Small potatoes junk for small potatoes dysfunction, I figured. Probably the kinds of smokers who moaned all evening about how their daddies wouldn't let them have the car. Poor boys. Such troubles teenagers had to contend with nowadays that it ran rampant over Facebook: My cell phone is broken. I have to work five whole hours today. FML.

Mind you: my head started to hang of its own accord as I got past them because I could hear my mother's voice in my head haranguing me over the issues I'd turned to junk for.

FML, indeed, if it had been a term five years earlier when I'd moved from digesting those small potato issues to the real meat of self-medication. Oh, yes. FML to the max.

Once inside, I eased into the dankness, letting the claustrophobic stink of old cigarette smoke, fried food, and stale beer settle into a space just behind my palette. I shimmied up to the counter close enough to the barkeep that I could catch her eye. I'd been a grade behind her in school but you don't go making statements about your sexuality as plainly as I did in those days in a town as small as ours and not draw attention. She was just about the only person to accept me then for what I was when most everyone else called me a SHIT: she/he/it abbreviated. It was a cute pun because I kept switching my gender to match what cues I thought I was experiencing, and the cleverness of it was something I would never have expected from narrow-minded teenagers.

I remember wanting to leave a pile of myself in their pillowcases while they slept.

"I need a Jack and ginger, Renée," I said to her, laying down a ten-dollar bill and leaning in so she could hear.

"A black what, J?" She slipped the bill off the bar counter and was already turning the change into quarters so I'd leave her most of it as a tip. "Didn't catch that."

Renée's mother was a French woman from up the same bay as Molly, and like Molly, while her English was perfect; she still had an accent from being spoken to in Acadian French till she started school. Her THs came out all lumped like a bit of dough.

I twitched my head in the direction of the various whiskeys. "Jack Daniels and ginger ale."

She went for the hard liquor shelf.

"Not too bad for a Friday night; no real bad dance crap yet," I said to her.

She looked askance at the owner who sat on a torn plastic bench at a nearby booth, hunched over a MacBook. "Not for long. He's culling out the play list." She pointed out the Crown Royal bottle and I shook my head, pointing to the black labeled one next to it.

She reached to pull down the Jack Daniels and her shirt fell back at the neck, revealing skin that sported a narrow violet bra strap. A sporty type demi cup bra, I figured. Maybe with some lace at the bottom, nice satin material with just enough sticky material on the closure that the bra would hold in place without riding up the back. My man's stomach made a pathetic chirp at the sight of it, and I tried to hush it to no avail. It took a long pull from the drink she gave me to stomp it down. I turned and looked out into the bar, resting my back against the tall stool, face to the crowd and away from the bar and sight of that gorgeous purple bra strap.

You see, relapses aren't just for addicts.

There was a time when the angels on my mother's shelves scolded me with their plaster eyes every time I put a purse to my shoulder. Then they out and out cheered when I threw that purse to the corner in disgust and pulled on a pair of tighty-whitey men's briefs. They liked it when my gender matched my genitalia. To be honest, I did too. It kept the arguments with myself at bay. But the comfort of not having to question what I was never lasted. The shifting of gender happened so often that I began to wonder if I was really transitioning from one gender to the other at all, or if I was just identifying stereotypical cues for the sake of drawing lines for myself that could put a label on what I was feeling.

The trouble with those signals was that I was suffering all of them in spans of 24 hours, of two hours, of one. I was making myself dizzy with the moving from one gender to the next: one minute I felt like downing a bolt of whiskey, the next I was running feathers across my shoulders, wondering if caffeine was really good for cellulite. It didn't make sense to me that I could swing so suddenly. Each time I told my mother I was a different sex, the little bastard eunuchs sat on their shelves and mocked me, them with no genitalia to worry about. Just wings to stretch and smiles to pull.

You have to understand: I'm not bi; I'm not gay. I'm straight. No matter what the gender, I present as a heterosexual human being, and thus is my shit-faced rage at the whole issue in the first place.

I end up walking both sides, teetering precariously from time to time because that line is a razor sharp one that has very little empathy when you're barefoot and vulnerable. Vulnerability sent me into a frenzy best left undescribed to the modern masses and so I'll spare you those details. The bar was one place where the darkness made it easier for me to be whatever the Hell I figured I was at the time.

So when a Tarzan holler came from somewhere in that dankness, I scoped out the semi-dark and saw two arms flailing from a booth on the left wall just as a head popped out from the side. Molly. She'd had her hair styled specially for the hometown, it seemed: a bristle of white spikes in a perfect imitation of a hedgehog's back but with alternating black and green tips.

As I threaded my way through the small groups of early partiers, I could see she'd put on a cravat beneath her black silk shirt.

I pushed into the booth opposite her. "You've had your hair done."

She shrugged as though the matter was inconsequential, but I saw her put her fingers to the back and touch one of the spikes.

"My hair is my strength you know."

"Oh, I imagine it gets you all kinds of action."

She looked at me, all serious for a gal whose hair bristled ridiculously. "Really," she said. "I'd be like Samson without my hair."

"Samson."

"And Delilah. Cut his hair. He dies."

"What movie is that from?"

I knew she'd been brought up Roman Catholic before her mother had started attending an Evangelical church in town, one where parishioners swung from the chandeliers and rolled down the aisles if the stories were true. When she'd told me all about it, it scared the bejesus out of me to think that a rational person could be so swayed by a sermon they could do such outrageous things. Still, it was fun to plead ignorance with her just for the reaction she'd give.

"Sheesh, for a Baptist you're awfully uninformed. It's from the Bible."

"Never saw it."

"You're pathetic." She pulled a face.

"So. What's on for tonight?"

"Well, so far the menu seems a little skimpy." She made a show of inspecting the room and put her finger to her lip in mock contemplation. "Still, I'm in the mood for redhead. I've been drinking a lot of red wine lately."

"Red with red, huh?"

She grinned. "I'm cultured."

"Right," I said. "I forgot how apropos you could be." I shot a quick glance around. "You won't find many gingers around here, though."

"You never know. I might get lucky."

"Not looking like that."

"Looking like what?" She pressed her chin into her chest where it doubled into a podge of skin. She turned left, turned right, inspecting. "What's wrong with how I look?"

"For starters, you look like Hugh Hefner."

"So? What's wrong with ole Hef? He gets girls all the time."

"He's a billionaire."

"And you think that's why he gets such hot chicks."

"It's the only reason any hot chick digs an old man."

"No, really," she said incredulous. "You don't think he has any charms left at all?"

"He's nasty looking. He could have just crawled out of the crypt keeper's ass."

"And you figure looking like that he must just be getting

women because of his money?"

"Why else?"

"Oh come on. No self-respecting woman would screw someone as old as that for mere money. No amount of money. There has to be something else."

"What kind of else would there be?"

She shrugged. "Maybe he just has some huge pile of charm."

"Or dick. Maybe he just has a huge dick."

"You always think it comes down to the dick."

"It does always come down to the dick," I said. "You just get huffy because you don't have one."

"I don't need one."

She said it with such vehemence, that I realized her trip home had been about more than coming to party with me. She came home because it did come down to the dick; she'd been dumped. Her penchant for straight women meant she would suffer abandonment eventually, when the would-be lesbians finished their experiment.

I reached for her hand across the table and stroked the back of it playfully. "You know they're not so bad, dicks. Do you ever wonder if I have one?"

"You just are a dick." She turned her hand over and grasped my fingers, giving them an equally playful, but painful squeeze for my trouble.

I grinned at her.

"So," I said, eyeing the clusters of ladies hovering near the dance floor. "Anyone look good to you? See anyone worthwhile?"

As a man, I'm not a six-foot Spartan warrior; I'm a five foot eight inch pretty boy with blond hair and what I've heard are piercing green eyes. Women love pretty boys when they're in their teens and are still in many ways not sure of their own sexual prowess. But women in their 20s? Well, they know what they want, and what they want is a Spartan warrior--at least that's what the feminine in me wants. I hoped there'd be someone here who could stand either.

Molly shrugged as she pulled her beer closer. "There was a gorgeous black girl here earlier." She craned her neck so she could see over the crowd huddled at the counter. "Yup. She's upending a Keith's. See her? Boobs spilling out her top?"

I did see her. She had to be at least five nine: an Amazon with python legs. Her skin awash in red light from the dance floor floods, making the deep brown seem like caramelized honey.

I took a deep breath.

"Pretty freaken' nice if you ask me. I might rethink my ginger hunt just for tonight." She took a pull from her beer then plopped it down on the gouged table and made a show of sighing theatrically. "One drink away from leaving catcher's position and strapping on the bat," she said.

"And we're off."

"Off?"

"Yeah, the reason you have so much trouble with women."

She out and out snorted as though to say she was ole Hef in the female flesh.

"I don't have any problems with women." She looked away as she said it and I ended up having to talk to her profile.

"Um, yeah; you do. Look at you now."

She picked at something beneath the table and brought up a hunk of gum. She grimaced and scraped it on the edge.

"Molly?"

She looked up. "I heard you."

"Well then?"

"Well nothing. It's not what you think, Jay; I'm not home because I'm sulking. Hell, I'm home to party."

"Sure, because someone dumped you. Some woman. Some straight woman you thought you'd change."

She downed the rest of her draft and plunked the bottle on the table. "I don't try to change them because there's nothing to change. Women just are lesbians at the core. They all are."

She leaned back, flung an arm over the back of the bench and avoided my eye, quite purposely, I thought. The black silk cravat shone red where the lights hit it.

I'd heard it before of course, always when she was feeling insecure. Always when she'd got dumped for a man and was feeling the rage that comes with abandonment. Always when she was on the prowl for a conquest, not a love interest.

We sat in uncomfortable silence. I stared into my whiskey, wishing I'd ordered something different, and she picked at her already bitten-to-the-quick nails. I waved at the server as she wandered close to the table and passed her a ten-dollar bill for two Coors: one for each of us. I drank half of mine in one upend and wished for a different drink still.

I watched the few servers threading their ways through the half dozen clusters of drinkers, watched them nod and amble away. A few young men, obviously just turned nineteen tried to look as though they'd been coming to the bar for simply ages, but gave themselves away in the furtive glances they made, open mouthed, agog at the beauty of the waitresses and the fact that those tightly clad, be-aproned lovelies would be bringing them libations.

"What the Hell are you looking at?"

It took me a second to realize Molly wasn't talking to me; she had swiveled her head in the direction of a petite bar patron with long hair and perky boobs. The girl held the stem of a martini glass in a delicate, manicured grasp, the white French tips of her nails catching shards of errant disco lights. She stared back at Molly with owlish eyes and a dropped jaw as Molly's voice got even louder.

"You never see a fucken dyke before?"

I grabbed for Molly's hand, trying to distract her before she, as usual, took things too far. "Molly," I said. "Molly?"

"What?" She turned back, fire in her gaze, and I knew she was already making a move toward that trip-too-far. "You know she was staring at me." She glared toward the girl who had flipped tail already and was threading her way through the crowd, trying to appear as though she hadn't been flagged.

Molly called out after her anyway. "Go buy yourself a Gucci purse or something. Or better yet, learn yourself some French." She put on a look of distaste. "Pubnicoers," she said.

"Molly."

"What?"

"You might want to ease off on your distaste for anything Pubnico."

"Why the Hell should I?"

"Because this place is crawling with people. Pubnicoers and Townies alike."

She scrunched her brows together. "So?"

"So, you should be more tolerant."

"Why the Hell should I be tolerant of a community that doesn't tolerate anything but money?"

I sighed. I'd known Molly for a long time, and I'd lived in between the two French communities for even longer. One thing I'd learned about Molly was her flat prejudice of any French community different than her own. Her distaste for Pubnico Acadian was very much based in the difference in accent and the way it differed from her own French Shore way of mangling the original French into something disdained by any Quebecois that visited the area. Each area thought their patois was superior to the other, and many English thought all of it was unintellgiible. A point of far reaching prejudice I thought I'd bring on home to her.

"Don't you think they might think the same about you?"

"What, you think they'd call me a fancy-assed priss pants that has to have the best of everything. Can't speak French. Can't speak English."

I couldn't help grinning. Not because she was right, of course because she wasn't, but because her accent was marring and removing all the THs from her words--a result of her own trouble speaking perfectly enunciated English.

She caught my smile.

"I fucken hate 'em," she said with a smile in her tone.

"I bet they hate you too."

"They better fucken hate me. I'm the queen of hate. Get it? Queen?"

"That would only apply if you were gay."

"I am gay."

"Men are gay, Molly. Chicks are lesbians. Plus: you don't even know she was from Pubnico."

"I do so. She has the look."

"Oh, yes. The Look." I shuddered playfully.

She blew through her lips, making a raspberry that sent spit across the table.

I chuckled. "Look at you. You can't keep your eyes off that girl's ass. So much for how much you hate folks from Pubnico." Prejudiced, she might be, but she did love a good ass. And I was beginning to think that anger was fueled by something more than her French-on-French prejudice.

She grinned and made a helpless gesture. "A bitch is a bitch." She got up and made to scan over the heads of the crowd. "Where'd she go, anyways?"

"She's there." I pointed her out as she stood next to a burly looking unshaven chunk of young man. She was attractive as many from that French quarter were; it helped that she sported a sparkling purple Vera Wang cocktail blouse, undoubtedly bought from eBay or during a yearly trip to New York. Molly could say what she would about girls from *Par en Bas*, they knew quality and they knew how to make that quality look damned good.

I caught the look on Molly's face and I knew what she was about to do even without her saying so.

"Don't go there," I told her.

"Just one drink."

"No," I said. "No drinks."

She ignored me, signaling for the server. "Can you send a beer over to that girl?" She pointed. "The one next to that behemoth?" She dug into her pocket and pulled out a ten-dollar bill. "Here," she said. "Keep the change, but make sure she knows who it came from."

The server nodded and made to thread her way back to the bar.

"Now," Molly said, "we wait."

"You're gonna get hurt."

"Hush. You don't know shit."

"She's wearing a Wang; what makes you think she's gonna drink beer?"

She spurted with sarcasm. "Because she's only *froufrou* on the outside. You know how it is: you can take the girl out of Pubnico, but you can't take Pubnico out of the girl."

She watched as the server moved closer to the girl with an opened bottle of ale. There was a short exchange that ended in the server pointing our way. I wanted to cringe out of sight; Molly waggled her fingers and blew a kiss.

"What do you think is going to happen?"

She shushed me. "Wait."

I did as I was bid, peering from beneath my palm. The girl accepted the beer, chugged mercilessly from it in one upend, and put it down purposefully on the nearest table. I wasn't surprised to see her position her back to us. Molly, it seemed, thought the finale would be much different.

"That bitch."

"You thought she'd come running into your arms?"

"I thought she'd thank me for the beer."

"Why do you care?"

"I don't." She leaned back in her seat. "I mean, she's the one missing out. Rock her world, baby. I'd rock her world." Then she muttered something about not being able to compete with a fisherman anyway, not enough money or some such, then turned brightly back to me. "Wanna follow her around?"

"You're twelve, right? Somehow time warped into the body of a twenty-something?"

"You're absolutely no fun."

"Ok. So we follow her around the bar, intimidate her. What's the point?"

She shrugged.

"And you say you don't have any problems with women."

"If I have troubles with women, what would you call the troubles you have, my freaky friend?"

"My troubles don't send me into fits of debauchery like yours do."

She quirked her brow sarcastically.

"They don't," I protested.

"How the mighty forget." She held up her fingers as though she were going to count down. I interrupted her before she could tick off the first finger.

"My troubles are an equal opportunity employer."

She nodded quickly. "You bet. You got more ripples in your ocean than a pond of frogs."

"That doesn't make any sense."

She shrugged, indicating that she didn't care if it made sense or not. "It would sound better in French." She tipped her bottle at me. "Down the hatch old man."

I tinked her bottle with mine. "To the trolls."

"To trolling." She guzzled down her brew and got up again. I watched as she threaded her way through the crowds till she'd positioned herself very close to the girl she'd been harassing. The girl appeared oblivious to the large dyke looming behind her as though she were a shadow about to merge with its owner. I shook my head. It always intrigued me to see Molly in action.

Chapter 2

I watched as Molly ran her hand up the spikes in her hair, making sure they bristled. She cozied closer to the girl, who was in animated conversation with a pudgy female patron gripping a beer bottle with both hands. The burly fisherman hung close. It was obvious he was trying to pass off the Keiths to the pretty Pubnicoer but couldn't get her attention away from her friend long enough for her to take it.

I watched as Molly slithered into the conversation with seeming ease. She laughed at something the fisherman said-- that got her in. She smiled at the pudgy girl, moved closer to the pudgy girl, touched the pudgy girl gently on the shoulder as she talked.

It didn't take long for the girl to accept a beer from Molly, who had already quartered her out from her companion and was giving her such deliberate attention that the Pubnico filly had taken notice. Molly had turned her back to the beauty and looked genuinely interested in the shorter one. She had her arm around her shoulder and they had begun to sing to an awful disco remake, their mouths opening wide. They laughed at each other. I couldn't help a chuckle myself when the Pubnico girl started studying Molly closely and tried to catch her friend's attention in an effort to make her way back into the conversation. The fisherman seemed all but forgotten.

I knew Molly's interest in the girl might have started out as retaliation for rejection, but I also knew it had shifted in the time she was there. Molly was an incurable extrovert. In minutes she was herding the girl outside, I knew, to share a cigarette laced with weed. It wouldn't be stronger--not yet. Stronger for Molly would come later, after she'd found someone to take home. She'd bring out the E when she knew it would be worth using and not a waste of her stash.

I sighed as I sat in the booth by myself. While I might hope that things had changed for Molly, I knew she was stuck treading metaphorical water; she enjoyed her lifestyle, and while she'd never gone as far under as I had, I worried that she wouldn't be able to keep her head up if she kept at it without rest.

I had another bottle of beer on the table before she found her way back, a paper clenched in her hand.

"Cell phone number," she said as she heaved herself onto the bench opposite me.

"So why not take her home?"

She shook her head. "She's not ready to trip the light Molly-fantastic yet. Besides, I'm out for a redhead tonight."

"You can be so picky, I suppose."

"Damn straight. You saw me."

"I haven't been so lucky."

"I can tell," she said. "You worked the room so hard from your spot at the table."

It was true. I'd done nothing. "I guess I must not be in the mood."

She waved her hand in the air, dismissing the comment. "You're just in a funk. Comes from being home."

I said nothing and she looked at me with deliberation.

"You're not thinking about using again?" She waggled her finger at me.

I gave her a hard look. "You're kidding me?"

She leaned back in the booth, crossing her arms and directing at me, a very stern look.

"Molly?"

It took a few seconds, but eventually she brightened and cast me a grin. It seemed as though she had got what she was looking for, that I had passed the test.

"Yeah, yeah," she said. "I'm joking. I know you're done with that shit. Just testing you."

"Well it makes me wonder at the credibility of the proctor when she's taking young girls out back for a smoke and God knows what else."

"What made you think I took her out for a smoke?"

"Maybe the stink of marijuana on your clothes?"

"She took me out, if you must know." She looked offended.

"Aren't you tired of that shit?"

"I seem to recall a certain someone rolling around in a muckier pigpen."

No sense arguing over who was going to fall hardest from their high horse, but dammit, I had earned some bit of respect from her. She knew how hard it had been for me. She knew. And here she was flaunting her own abuse in front of me. Making the skin on my forearms pimple in unwanted memory.

"Do you know what I think?"

She lifted a thick black brow. "What do you think?"

"I think you want me to fail."

She put her hand to her chest where I knew she had her ample boobs strapped flat. "That's not true, and you know it."

"Do I?"

"Of course you know it. How can you say that, Jay?"

"I'm not sure I like the way you say my name."

"The way I say your name? What are you talking about?"

"You say J like it's got more than one letter. Like you're making an effort to pronounce vowels that aren't there."

The bar was beginning to show signs of filling up. The clusters of people had grown and somewhere to my side I could hear the shrill laugh of an already drunken woman. The music crept up and I looked at Molly who had crossed her arms so hard I could see the boob fat being squashed down beneath the pressure.

"Well what do you expect? You never know whether you're a man or woman. How do you expect people to react? How are they supposed to know what kind of identity you've decided to go by? Your so-called gender identity changes as much as I change lovers."

I didn't like the way she stressed the word identity or the way she stuck her fingers into the air to pull those damn quotes from the ether. I made a grab for her fingers and held them, closed tightly together, maybe pinching them just a little, maybe pinching them just a little harder than I intended.

"Underwear," I said." You mean underwear. You change lovers like you change underwear. Indicates you're easy."

She sputtered like an old engine. "I am easy. In fact, if I wasn't so queer, I think I'd be a slut."

She extricated her fingers from my grasp and twirled one of the green-tipped spikes indicating she knew she'd hobbled into some tar pit, and was trying to use her humor, unsuccessfully, as a piece of hemp rope to pull her out. "Don't be mad, Jay. Come on. Let's talk about something else. I hate it when we fight."

"No, you come on," I told her. "You do that all the time and I hate it."

"Well, it's not like you were born with both sex parts; you were born with one."

"I was born a natal man, yes." My answer was wary.

"So you can't be trans all the time," she said. "I mean, when you're in your real body, you're just regular ole Jay. Straight Jay at that." She made a great show of sounding disgusted. The intent was a teasing one, but I didn't take it that way.

"It's J, Molly. Short and perfunctory. And you don't know what you're talking about."

"Oh, look who's using words he doesn't think I'll understand. But I do. You know I do."

"Perfunctory isn't that incomprehensible a word."

"No. Not that. What we were talking about. I get it. I

do. It's you who isn't getting it. Look: were you born a he/she?" She waited for a response that I wouldn't give before answering her own question. "See? You're only trans--at the best of times--half the time. The other half, you're just plain ole heterosexual."

She'd evidently just worked out Einstein's dodgy Universal Theory. I'd certainly heard the argument before, of course, most of them from queers. Nothing like a special community to nail down exactly where their specialty lines fell.

She grinned. "So it's good for you; you fit in sometimes. Cheer up. That means you're normal."

"Normal."

"Yeah. You know, that old: do-you-think-I'd-choose-to-be-gay-with-all-the-discrimination argument."

"But I'm not gay."

She pressed her bottom lip into the top, considering. "You sit on the fence all the time. You're not like a real gay person who has no choice, who's always going to have to deal with prejudice. You're not like us. We have to fight to get married, to get a good job, to get plain old respect for Jesus sake. We have to take the world's hit, but you? You can pass. When you're in your right gender, there's no reason for anyone to discriminate against you."

All this as if my sex parts had anything to do with my gender. Once I suppose it hadn't mattered to me; maybe during that androgynous time when my mother didn't care if I carried a doll or rammed a truck into a cupboard. When I dressed in sweat pants and T-shirts and it didn't matter because I was getting my clothes dirty and no one, absolutely no one, was outdoors with me expecting me to act one way or another except that I be friendly. Back when I, like every kid, understood the dance of play. I think then I was happy. I think then I knew what I was: a kid. Just a kid.

The very fact that she said gender--singular--meant she didn't get it, just like the rest of the sanctimonious gay community she hung out with on the weekends, pretending

S&M was a dog-eared fit into the lifestyle, acting as though debauchery was part of the lifestyle like oil was part of peanut butter. For all her wisdom in areas LGB, she wasn't all that educated in the T.

"Fuck it," I said out loud and let the ever-growing loudness of the music embrace me. "Go find your ginger girl. I don't give a shit what you do or who you do it with."

I got up and looked down at her, pulling her cravat loose and shaking my head. "Call me when you grow up."

I started working my way back to the bar; I should have ordered a Long Island iced tea, that's what I should have done. I started digging into my wallet, hoping for a couple of twenties and thinking I should just empty the whole freaking thing and drop the leather into a waste bin. It was ugly, plain, and simple. I'd thought it perfectly functional when I bought it. Now, I hated that same functionality.

I pressed my way closer to the bar. Things really were getting busy. I'd got in easier when I'd first arrived; now I had to bat my eyelashes at every fisherman hanging close in stinking coveralls--they backed off as though they'd been burnt. The metro sexual, cologne-wearing guys gave me glares for my trouble, but they too made room.

"What's she drinking, Renée?" I asked the barkeep when I made it nearly to the edge. "You know the gal with the boobs over there?" I pointed out the lovely black girl who was heading just then to the ladies' room. With glee, I discovered Dame Fortune was with me; I fumbled out a fifty. "Never mind. Just get me a Long Island."

"Fucken queers," I muttered to myself. Who were they to decide what side of the lines to color on? I looked up from the bills in my hand to see Renée shaking her head, mouthing something I couldn't make out over the now deafening music.

I had to squeeze between two beefy fishermen to hear her. "What do you mean, no?"

She eased a mug off the tap and raised her voice. "You think all women drink those damned things."

"It's for me," I told her.

She cocked a manicured black brow. "I dunno..."

"No, really. Pour me one." I did a shoulder check toward the ladies' room. Just seeing the glimpse of stalls as the door swung shut was enough to make my bladder twitch. I thought better of the drink. "Hold on. I'll be back for it; I gotta pee."

I had to ease myself through the clusters of bar flies that congregated around the bar and video lottery machines close to the bathrooms. I noticed a young man, maybe in his mid-twenties catch my eye. I shot him a shy grin and made for the door of the ladies' room. The door had a copper push plate with a patina that had more to do with generations of palm grease than sophisticated aging. I pressed my elbow into it and shoved.

The girl I'd haunted earlier stood by the sink, ring finger smoothing the hollows beneath her eyes. I ran my hands down the sides of my shirt and cast around for a good opening. Surely, the quick pee could wait if I could grab a chance to introduce myself. She caught sight of me in the mirror.

"What the fuck?" she said in a tone much shriller than I'd expected from such a large chest. "Get the Hell out of here."

I caught my own eye over her shoulder in the mirror and jangled around for a response that would be cogent and came up empty as a vacuum. Like a cog of a machine rattling lose, a piece of logic clanked onto the floor of my mind and spun on its end. To my left, I heard a bathroom door thunk shut and a squeal of surprise come from whoever was exiting the stall.

The black girl advanced on me, her mouth moving in curses I'd imagine would make a grizzled fisherman hang his head in disgrace; her gaze angry, finger in my face then on my chest, poking me, drilling into the hard bone of my sternum. Something jolted awake beneath it and beat its wings in alarm.

"Get the fuck out." That skin, so like caramelized honey

on the dance floor up close was flushed beneath the mocha. I felt trapped, my feet mired in the stickiness of confusion.

I was ten again. Bully in the bathroom. Sick with fear. Trying to speak, to appease, to do something that would deflect the fists I knew would come. I felt nauseous with revulsion and shame because I remembered I'd pissed myself then; I hated to revisit that now, the hot scent of urine was nothing to the shame of it, and while the sense of wetness was easy to forget, the puddle in my psyche would never dry. I felt it sopping again now into my consciousness.

"Sorry," I stammered. "Wrong door." Funny. It was always the wrong door.

Chapter 3

I struggled toward the exit, fighting my feet and feeling as though I was wearing heels too high to walk right, too spiked to keep my balance. I've often found solace in shoes, but not at that moment. Even the black Converse I was wearing didn't feel grounded enough. I found the door and yanked the handle, not seeing anything distinct in the outlying bar, only shapes and colors through the water that stung my eyes. Knowing I was crying only made the sensation of confusion worse. I had to choke on the sounds that wanted out of my throat. I headed blindly for the red blur of the exit sign.

The solidity of a chest stopped my progress to the door. It was hard. Male, undoubtedly, yet it yielded momentarily, awkwardly. I was reminded of the time a jock mistook me for a young woman on the city transit bus and offered me his seat. I didn't argue then, just blessed the mistaken identity and settled in, secure in my homeward trek, looking forward to my cat and my TV dinner.

Fingers clenched my arm to steady me, bringing me back to where I was, and I looked up into an unfamiliar face.

"Sorry," I said to the Adam's apple.

That face, handsome in a rough way, showing concern at first as it angled down to catch my eye, tracked into an irritated expression at having been duped into showing a minute of concern for what he'd obviously thought was a woman.

"No worries," he said but when I started to move aside he blocked me again. My stomach flipped over on itself: I'd been here before. Some men, despite my male appearance, somehow knew I wasn't their kind of masculine.

"I just want out," I said.

"Sure, sure," he answered, but he didn't move.

I snuffled up the tears and snot that had crept traitorously out upon my exit from the ladies' room, hoarding the fluids in response to the threat in the air. If I kept my cool, I'd get out, get home, put on a nice silk nightgown and go to bed. No animals harmed in the episode. I sidestepped to the left and pressed forward--into muscle. The feel of it made me think of the futility of time trying to erode the pyramids.

"You know what? I'm pretty tired." I didn't even look up again, but sort of mumbled the words into his chest. It was true. I was tired. Sick and tired and fed up with bullshit.

I sighed theatrically, unable to keep myself from doing it. "I just want to go home."

"You wanna go home with a woman or a man, pretty boy?"

I took a short breath in response to the question. So the die had been rolled after all, and I wasn't going to get out without some sort of cruelty. Probably physical. Probably physically painful. It was always this way; probably always would be.

I looked up then, straight into eyes too blue to be unaided by colored contacts, with lashes made of two black feathers. I foolishly tried on the best imitation of him I could muster.

"Why?" I said. "You wanna go home with a pretty boy?"

I batted my eyelashes at him, thinking even as I did so, that I was a complete idiot. I mean, how else was it going to turn out except for the very large man to take out his latent homosexual fears on the youthful, misunderstood pretty boy? I didn't get more than three blinks when all the air in my lungs was forced out from the gut up. My stomach doubled over his fist, my hands pressed in to protect it, feeling certain the booze that was in there would shortly be all over his shoes. Before the bile could rise from its strangled spot in my gullet to my throat, I was being shuffled along by a series of hands and thighs.

I knew there were at least four of them; dimly I knew there could be more. I'd been in the position enough over the years that I knew I was being pushed along from beneath the cover of half a dozen homophobic men--for whatever personal reasons they would have to want to beat the living, breathing, flouncing life out of me. The bouncers at the door either wouldn't see or wouldn't care.

The pave of the parking lot had a black sheen from the recent rain, the streetlights and signs from nearby shops reflected and diffused out over the surface, making a colorful carpet of reds and yellows, of contusion purples. I stumbled into a puddle, watched the rings of waves distort the picture. It was a sight I knew I'd remember long after the pain of inevitable bruises left my body. The music from inside leaked out through the walls: Pink, I thought foolishly, singing about coming up to a party. I couldn't help a chuckle. Some party.

The human roadblock to home lifted me to my feet, gripped me beneath the chin, cradling it like he was about to kiss a desirable woman.

"What's up with you, gayboy? What's so funny?"

Seeing as I was already doubled over, it seemed fitting in a way that I kept chuckling, uncontrollably in time with the spasms of shudders that had taken over my entire body. Oh, stupid body, did it not know what was about to happen to it, for it to shake with laughter at such a time?

He stepped closer. I could smell Lacoste, imagine the alligator on the bottle with its mouth open. I forced the ridiculous vision of this bully leaping like the actor in the commercial, across one wharf pole to the other, white pants forming folds against the wind, green polo shirt molded against his abs. One lord a-leaping. So ordinary. So metrosexual. I held onto it, that image. Made him jump in my mind from pylon to pylon over and over.

His voice came again and he sounded angrier to think that I'd not be trembling from his threatening voice, the boom in it, the demand that I quake before him. "You think it's funny getting the shit kicked outta ya?"

If he only knew how often I'd heard those words. I felt almost sorry for him: his ignorance, his fear. I heard my teeth clacking together and punctuating my words in a peculiar way. An odd way to laugh, I thought.

"You beat on women much?" I managed.

"Fuck," he said, disgusted. "You got yourself some troubles if you're a woman with that much stubble."

He looked over to one of his buddies with leather thong flipflops on his meaty feet. At least I knew that guy wouldn't be kicking me when the token banter was finished and they set about, finally, to what they were after. That first fellow? Well, you know how these things always end up. He'd come out prepared for a shitkicking, dressed for it almost subconsciously like so many loud-mouthed bullies do. I stole a peek to see exactly how sturdy his Cat shoes looked and came away with a dead certainty of how much weight they could heft into my belly.

The ringleader spoke to the flip-flop guy, adding just enough camaraderie to his voice that any passersby would figure it was nothing but light conversation. "Sonny," he said to him, "you ever see a woman with that much beard."

"Not on her face," Sonny said and nodded, laughing at his own joke. I found myself laughing too. It was funny, after all.

"Not on her face," the first man repeated, shoving his hands into his pockets. I saw his bicep move beneath his shirt. Nobody in their right or combative mind would stick their hands in their pockets if they planned to meld their flesh into your face. They'd need them out, to the ready, snarled into fists and eager to go. For a second I thought I might get away with a few insults after all.

The laughter died in my throat. I felt the undeniable

quake of apathy take over my limbs, stilling them. When he came out of his jeans pockets with a small knife, I knew I was in for more than the typical scuffle. I think I choked then. I know I coughed uncontrollably, and I'm not sure if it was because of the kick to the kidneys that Sonny delivered before he grabbed hold of my balls or because I'd swallowed my own spit down wrong.

As beatings go, it wasn't the worst I've ever suffered: a long wet line drawn down my jaw, a few nicks, a painful, sometimes blood- lubricated dry shave as I stood held against my will by Sonny's fingers clenched around my scrotum. He seemed to take a particular glee in squeezing it till my breath left my body and pains shot up to my ribcage.

Each time a spasm came, I called them all the gay names I could think of as the air exited my lungs: cocksuckers, fruits, freaks; I gave them all back, damn them. Every curse was a mantra. And when a few kicks in the back, a few beltings to the ribs, and one or two stomps on my shoulder later, they released me to the pave, a fetal positioned pretty boy as far as they knew clutching his ribs, I took a suffragette pride that I'd not gone down simpering.

So no, even though the thought that I might die came with each advance of the blade, it still wasn't the worst pounding. Nor was it the worst that they called me freak and gayboy and goddamned devil bait: well, granted devil bait was new, but I was used to the others. No. None of that was the worst I'd been through physically.

Maybe you would think I've lost all my marbles in the process because a beating's a beating, and a beating's always painful. Maybe you've never had a beating. Maybe you've always been the beater, but I'm here to tell you: there's something about seeing a flash of silver making its way toward your face that bruises you in ways you can never explain. Each time the knife scraped down my chin, grazing off the minutiae of stubble and catching on each hair, pulling, I held my breath and hoped the blade wouldn't slip onto the tender parts of my throat. And more than that, I almost wanted it to. I wanted out in that moment. No survival instinct came to my aid to make me beg for mercy. It was as though the primal force of life had left me in that instant and I was glad for it. Glad, by God, because if they killed me, they'd suffer then. Oh, how they'd suffer.

And so you think that's a bad beating, I know. Most people would. But it was the shame of feeling Sonny's fingers clasped around my genitalia that hurt the most; not because it's a sensitive area and because the pressure of his fingers clawing deep into the folds of skin made some deep part of my stomach turn itself inside out. Because I wished in that moment that I had no genitalia, and the knowledge that I did was a streak of lightening in a dark sky, one that ripped into my very cells and sent jolts every which way, seeking a ground that didn't exist. The pain of that charge, that I had genitalia, male genitalia, electrified that familiar and corresponding ripple of shame I'd felt since my mother first caught me carrying around one of her old purses.

They left me in the same puddle that reflected the bar's sign in such brilliant colors when I'd first fallen, with muffled music in my ears, and the taste of car oil in my mouth. I lay on the pave for some time with my shoulder in the wet, my legs off to the side somewhere where I could feel that they were falling asleep but didn't have the energy to pull them back straight. No one came out of the club to smoke or to grab a taxi. Some part of my mind wondered if I was actually there, or if I'd melded into some parallel universe where club people didn't smoke or stumble drunkenly to their cars but stayed inside and partied for eternity.

Finally, though, when I thought I couldn't lie there any longer but wasn't sure I had the strength to lift myself up and take myself home the door to the bar opened and I saw high heeled feet clomp over to where I lay.

"Holy fuck," the owner of those feet said. "You okay?"

"It's just a scratch," I said and mustered enough energy

to push onto my side.

She gave a sharp intake of breath. "Jesus, It's you."

"That's the first time I've been mistaken for Christ." I looked up at her, my mocha beauty from the bathroom, saw in her expression a true compassion I'd not have hoped for a minute earlier. I lost the will to keep my eyes open.

"Come on." She put her warm hands beneath my shoulders and eased me gently so I slumped forward, over my legs. I felt her palm on my cheek, wiping off what I supposed was blood because my neck felt wet where it hadn't before. "Jesus, you've got to help me at least."

"Just call me J," I said. The effort to get to my knees, let alone my feet, was making my lungs hurt. "I'm not such a formal kind of god."

"You're gonna go to Hell for that."

"I think I've already been."

With her help, I managed to get to my feet, although my knees were shaky and my step was weak. She helped me to the curb where I could at least sit on something dry. I watched her pull a cell phone from her rhinestone-studded purse.

"It's okay. I don't need the police."

"No police," she said. "Cab. I'd take you to OutPatients myself, but I've had too much to drink."

"Oh," I said weakly. I supposed I did need a doctor. My lungs hurt and if I hadn't collapsed one in, I'd at least broken a rib.

I heard her give the address and then she flipped her phone closed.

"Thanks," I remembered to say.

She looked down at me. "No worries. Cab should be along soon."

I nodded.

"You think you need me to go with you?"

"No. I'm good."

"You don't look good."

"I am. Really. I've had worse."

"Had worse than this? A real scrapper, you must be," she said, but her voice didn't sound convinced.

"A real heavy bag more like it."

"You sound kind of wheezy."

"Probably my lung."

"Nah, not the lung. If it was collapsed, you'd be in worse shape."

I looked up at her.

"Well, not like you aren't in bad shape now, just that you'd not be able to breathe let alone talk if there was a problem with your lung. You'll need some stitches, though."

"And you know this?"

She sat down next to me. "It doesn't take a doctor to see you need stitches." She splayed her legs out along the pave and brushed along the back of my ear with her fingers. She rubbed them together and wiped something brownish on her jeans leg. When she spoke again, it was with a measure of pride. "I've got one month left before I finish my LPN."

"Good for you," I said and tried to smile. The act of making room for her next to me shot a zinger down my side. She must have seen me wince and responded in a cold, diagnostic manner. Practicing, I supposed.

"It's probably a rib. Bruised up bad, maybe, but I doubt it's broken."

"How comforting."

She said nothing to that, and I couldn't find it in me to make more small talk. The effort of acting as though the beating hadn't shaken me up or hurt me was almost as exhausting as trying to fend off the blows in the first place.

I felt her palm on my waist. "I'm Sherona," she said. "Sorry about before; I don't usually curse like that."

I shrugged, thinking avoidance was the best decision. "It's okay. I shouldn't have gone in. I don't know what I was thinking."

She chortled. "Thinking you were gonna get laid or something, I imagine."

I faked a laugh. "Yeah," I said. "Something like that."

"You know, I can go with you to the hospital if you like, really. I don't mind."

I shook my head. "No. It's better if you don't."

"Better?"

"Easier, then." I watched as a taxi pulled into the parking lot. "I do appreciate your help, though. It was real good of you. You didn't have to do that."

"It was nothing," she said. "Anyone would do the same."

"Not everyone."

She squeezed my waist tighter, using the leverage to help me ease to my feet. "Anyone with a conscience," she said.

"Thanks for having one, then," I said and reached for the door, leaning in as much as I could to talk to the driver. "Hospital." I patted her hand when the driver nodded and clicked the meter onto start. "Thanks, Sherona--for everything."

She helped me shift my weight onto the car seat in the back. "No problem, J. Listen, you need me to make a statement or anything? You plan to press charges?"

I shook my head. Press charges and meet a worse beating the next time? I'd been through that before. I'd ended up having to move away from home to the city; but even being a misfit in my hometown didn't make the city that much more of fit for me. I was a small town person in a big city body. I'd been back for about six months, and had obviously forgotten how painful small town prejudice could be.

"I'll be fine. He'll forget all about me by tomorrow," I told her.

"Let's hope so," she said then shifted her posture as she shifted thought. "Well, sorry to have to meet you this way, J."

The driver grunted his impatience. She begged the driver to hold on for one more minute while she scribbled something on the back of a cash register receipt then shoved it in my front jean pocket. "My number," she said, "in case you need me...you know, for anything." She touched the edge of my cheek where it felt warm and wet. Then she slammed the door shut and blew me a kiss.

There are certain things that make a person feel more ashamed and guilty than anything else in the world. Lying to your mother and knowing she's going to find out and be disappointed. Gossiping about your best friend. Masturbating in a church bathroom after you've used up the last of the grocery and rent money for crank and then had to beg for cash from your parents on a Sunday morning: yeah. Those things are nearly unforgivable. But everyone has a monkey of some species on his back. I'd done all those things and while they'd made me feel pretty doggone guilty at the time, and sometimes for a long while after, there's never any match for the sense of guilt I feel for absolutely no reason at all. This girl's decency made me feel ashamed of myself. I didn't feel worthy. It left me wanting to make up for something that I'd never done to her. I felt dirty and indecent. I wanted to strip off my skin and leave nothing but the essence of myself because everything, from my hair to my toenails, was artificial.

Chapter 4

The hospital triage nurse had a mouth that looked like she'd bitten into a rancid lemon. Her skin was oiled and the one great age spot she had covered the bridge of her nose in what looked like a moth. She signed me into the registration desk by name and MSI card; I knew from experience she would not ask my sex.

"I'm femme," I said to her, knowing she'd have to check off sex, and knowing what she'd pick.

She looked up. "What?"

"I'm a woman. Put down female for gender."

"I don't have time for foolishness. I have a waiting room full of people."

I shot her what I hoped would look like a sincere grin, while focusing my eyes on the moth-eaten age spot. "I don't think the good doctor will have to know if I have ovaries or not to stitch a wound," I said.

Her tone in reply would have burnt my tender toes had it been a bath. "You don't think the physician will need to know if he has to worry about pregnancy or ruptured testes?"

"I would think if the doctor was a good one, he'd be able to treat the patient's symptoms by what he finds on the body, not by a check mark on a form." There went my mouth again. I'd probably get in to see the doctor just about when the plague broke out.

They let me in ahead of a toddler throwing up into a plastic bag. The doctor was young; he might have just graduated a month earlier. Middle Eastern, I thought. His skin had a pallor that suggested Pakistani or Indian, and his black gaze flitted over me in four seconds flat.

His accent had the odd, clipped resonance that led me to believe I'd guessed correctly. "You've had a nasty beating."

I nodded. I imagined he spent all his University evenings in the books to manage that kind of acuity so quickly into an appointment.

"Take off your shirt, please." He turned his back to me as he fiddled at the counter and came back around with a stethoscope wrapped around his neck and a jug of Sterigel in his hand. "We'll have to see if anything's cracked in there."

His exam was quick, fingers fleeting and soft as he poked and massaged. I doubted from time to time that he knew what he was doing because there was the barest minimum of pain from his exam. I almost felt cheated until I caught his gaze and the sympathetic message in it. The sight of it sent my gaze to my fingernails.

"Well," he said finally with a quick grin. "Nothing seems broken. Just badly bruised, mostly. I'll send you to X-Ray." He glanced pointedly at the scars on my torso.

"You've had a hard go, eh?"

I knew he meant more than the beating. I shrugged the best I could.

He waited a moment more, his gaze traveling to the faint silver line on my neck that I knew was there; he stayed on it for a moment, his lips pursed, then he seemed to give up.

"We'll just have to clean up the cuts some. They might infect and that'd be nasty. This one here," he pointed to the side of my head somewhere that I couldn't see." This one needs stitches."

I nodded again, relieved. "Sherona will make a fine nurse."

"Who?"

"Nothing," I said.

He crossed his arms and splayed his legs, bracing, it seemed, to deliver bad news. "You need an RCMP officer?"

I shook my head. "No." I eased myself down onto the examination table so I could lie flat. Stitches in the face would undoubtedly make me want to faint: easier if I was already lying down.

I felt his palm on my chest as he looked down at me. "I could phone them myself."

I shook my head.

"Ok, then." He retracted his hand and it felt cool where his hand had been. "It's going to hurt for a few days, I'm afraid."

"Quite a few," I said.

His voice came between rattlings of instruments in a silver tray. "Try some Advil tablets to help manage it."

I chuckled. "Yeah, sure. That'll help."

"If it doesn't, you can make an appointment with your regular doctor. He might decide to prescribe something stronger." He brandished a needle and his eyes crossed as he stared at the tip, making sure the syringe had no air bubbles.

"I don't have a regular doctor. And I think I'll stay away from stronger."

"Ah," he said. "There's a lot of you around here. With no doctor, I mean." He frowned and then lit up happily, giving away exactly how fresh he was from University. Maybe even a little uneducated still in the appropriate behavior department. Book smart, world wise, and socially inept. I liked him very much, right then.

"This is going to sting a little."

He took his time pulling stitches through some skin near my ear and the burn of the needle hooking through flesh not fully numbed made me forget the ache in my side, at least until he was done. When it was over, he pulled his pen out from his pocket and wrote on a slip of paper. "I'm just setting up practice. I don't have an assistant or a receptionist yet."

The paper had a number on it and his name: Bashir. "The stitches should dissolve on their own, but if you have any troubles, you call me in a day or so. I get off nights in

Emerg tomorrow, so I'm in my office day after that."

I took the paper, wishing I'd brought a purse or something to put it into. I pocketed it instead. "Thank you."

I eased my arm into my shirt and buttoned up. X-Ray let me in right away, and within another hour, I was free to go. Badly bruised and stitched, but free to go.

It was a good twenty-minute walk to my apartment from the bar, which meant at least another twenty minutes from the hospital. I checked my watch: 1:38 am. I hoped the cab service would still be running. In the city, it doesn't stop; in a small town, you can never be too sure. If you live in a small town, you realize there's either very little to do except drink, thus ensuring cab service at virtually all hours, or there's that insufferable attitude that you should do something better with your life than spend it imbibing cocktails during the wee hours of the day--thus rendering cab service the devil's handmaiden.

When I'd left, the town was in the throes of the first notion, with the added excitement of crack and coke and smack finding their way into the arena, so I imagined if all was the same, I'd manage a cab pretty easily.

I found myself digging into my pocket for change as I left Emergency.

The phone booth had somehow lost its telephone book, but some cab company had thoughtfully taped a business card to the side of the phone. I dialed the number, breath caught, hoping someone would answer who could save me a long, painful walk home.

"Seaside Taxi."

Ah. Blessed God. "I need a cab," I said into the receiver.

"No kidding," the other end drawled. "Where you goin'?"

Seemed the town had taken on some big city attitude, but I didn't have the luxury of arguing. "Seven Horton Street."

"Where you at?"

"Emergency."

"Ok. Five minutes."

I hung up, thanking whatever angel had decided to take my number that day. Five minutes was nothing. I could do five minutes, although the five minutes stretched into fifteen and the fifteen felt like a thousand, eventually, the cab did come and I could be grateful that I'd still get home long before than if I'd have walked. I got in, pressed twenty dollars into the driver's skinny fist, and laid back hoping there'd be no need for polite conversation until my apartment came into view.

You would know if you've ever been in a small Nova Scotian town, that such a thing isn't possible. They care too much there. They make conversation, open doors. Ask after your welfare.

I tried to keep my eyes downcast.

"Wow, buddy." The cab driver craned straight around in his seat to look at me. "You're a mess." It was a query, an invitation for me to regale him with the story of how I got that way.

"Indeed," I said, still keeping my gaze on my lap. "You've got the address."

I pressed back into the seat, hoping no more banter would be needed. He grunted with that equally infuriating sense that he knew when to pull his nose back out of someone's business. I wasn't sure why I felt cheated just then, only that when I got the silence I asked for, I brooded over it. When he pulled into my drive I leaned ahead so he could hear me well.

"You can keep whatever's left over." As payment for his small town conscience.

I climbed out, thinking that everything would be just fine if I could make it to my bed. I'd crawl into a ball right on top of the blankets and lie there until the world came to an end and I could ascend with the angels into a heaven where the lamb could lie with the lion and have its wounds licked.

Chapter 5

I slept the sleep of a prophet on his second day dead, straight through fourteen hours and what was usually the alarm of the infant's early morning shrieks from the apartment conjoined to mine. I missed its four and six am feedings, its diaper change and consequent feeding and nap at eight am, its exhausted need for a good-sized kink at two pm, and its endless wailing throughout all the periods in between and after. If you've lived next door to an infant suffering colic, in an apartment with wallpaper thin walls, you learn to schedule yourself around its round the clock hollering. I heard nothing till I woke with my hand on the angular slope of my hipbone at four pm Sunday afternoon.

While I felt far from refreshed, I did feel sort of like I was rising on the third day. There was an elation that I'd somehow barefooted my way across the hot coals of Hell into a small, very small, oasis. The bedroom was bright; I'd forgotten to pull the drapes and the full afternoon sun, a western light for my apartment, drenched the bed. I soaked it in for a few moments, turning so the sunlight could warm my face and so I could see out the window. The leaves of the oak tree next to the building played shadows on the beige bedspread.

It was only the ache in my bladder that set me out of bed and into the bathroom. My joints complained with each movement it took to get off the mattress and stumble, palms against the wall the entire way, to the bathroom. I sat on the seat, letting loose the pain in my bladder and staring down at my feet. I'd have to wax the hairs on top today if I planned to go out anywhere, paint the nails. Even if I didn't feel up to going out, there was no way I could look at all that hair and feel good about myself. I spared a thought for my armpits while I was at it. I'd have to wax there too. And my legs. And my bikini line. And my jaw.

It would be a lot of work; I felt along my ribcage and winced. I let my fingers trail across my chest and they came away sticky. Lube left over, obviously, from the doctor's fleeting exam.

Maybe waxing was too much work, too much stretching into awkward contortions, for the moment. You might think that as a woman, I'm an uber-feminine cross dresser going all out to look as much like a woman as possible. It's quite the opposite for me. I like feeling feminine, sure, but I'm not anal retentive about having my nails done or my makeup on all the time. The artifice is more a necessity if I'm going to call myself a woman: a diversionary tactic to draw the eye away from the chunk of Adam's apple. It's just that sometimes the eye that needs a diversion is my own. So as much as I didn't relish the thought of letting all that hair jungle its way into five pm, I really had little choice.

I needed a distraction.

I dabbed the tip of my penis with tissue and eased myself up. I'd splash some water on my face and maybe moisturize, then I'd log on to Facebook, maybe write an entry for my blog, that for all its excitement of going up six months ago, had taken a licking of its own in terms of my regularity.

I found it difficult to write the hard-nosed, black and white scribblings of someone who is uni-gender. *Oh woe is me, I'm MTF and I don't know if I should get reassignment surgery. I hate my penis. I want breasts.* There was plenty of that on the Internet. And not that it wasn't necessary for some to say, think, and find that shit, but for me, I'd passed that. At least I hoped so.

Since I'd be stuck inside for the day, I might as well reacquaint myself with the world of the Internet. I ran water into the sink, cold only, and splooshed my palms into the pool. I selected the softest hand towel I owned from the shelf next to the vanity and patted my skin delicately, taking extra care around my right eye, which was sore.

What greeted me in the mirror was enough to make me gasp, and the act of gasping sent a screech of pain down my neck. I looked more like a cadaver than a risen prophet. The right eye that felt like tenderized steak had a cut beneath that stretched from corner to nose. Blood still caked in what looked like a bug in the farthest corner toward my ear where the stitches were black and twisted. My cheekbone on that side looked bruised, and the right side of my jaw showed a swelling that explained the hard time I had opening my mouth. I didn't think I wanted to know how the rest of me looked when seeing the actual damage to my face made it hurt all the more.

I swallowed down the water that flooded my mouth and tried to gingerly brush aside what came to my eyes. I made an attempt to keep my eye on the faint thread of line where Doctor Bashir had let his own gaze linger. He'd wondered what it was from, I knew. He could discount the other, older scars, suspecting from my presence in Emerg how they must have been inflicted. He wouldn't have seen the track marks between my toes, behind my knees, or on the inside of my groin. Only the others; a jagged single incher on my forearm, an old circular burn scar on my chest, even a triple flicker on my lower belly, and a chorus of them up my ribcage: all horizontal like marching soldiers to a battle in the undergrowth: they'd all point to attacks of some sort. For him they would, at least.

I knew better.

I let my fingertip trace the fresh cut down my jawline to where it disappeared beneath the collar of my bloodied shirt. I could feel the awkwardness of my heartbeat, not because of the individual beats slamming into its surrounding viscera, but because my chest felt suddenly too small to contain it. Stupid ignorant fools. Did they think they could hurt the real me, when I hadn't been able to do enough damage myself?

I gripped the sink and let the tears come as silently and as gently as I could. And that act of trying to let go while holding myself calm enough not to hurt myself, felt all the more agonizing, because there was no satisfaction in it. No real release. I was as vacuous when I was done as the sink sounded when I pulled the plug.

To Hell with my gender blog; what use was a two dimensional navel-gazing, self-indulgent, lit screen about an issue that had caused me nothing but grief my entire life.

My bed called to me, and when I finally made it, panting by the time I sat down on it, I lay back and stared at the ceiling. There were thirty-two ceiling tiles above me. Five of them had water stains in brown shapes that could double as psychiatric inkblots. What remained had stickers on them of all sorts: a spaceship, a frog with a thought bubble next to his outstretched tongue that said, "Ribbit", and balloons and stars and butterflies, all in various states of peeling that told me that the person who occupied this apartment before had had children. I was sleeping in a child's room. Well, to be honest with you, I did feel pretty small.

I rolled over to face the wall. Sleep would come if I willed it. If I imagined my ribs didn't hurt, if I pretended my face didn't, if I told myself that everything was fine. I hadn't gone out last night. I hadn't left town. I hadn't been born. Sure. Sleep could relieve me from all that. Change it.

I concentrated. I imagined there was a hollow of black behind my eyes and nothing else. I tried to meter out my breath so that it spilled into the hollow and felt myself easing through the lack of color into the abyss.

I rolled onto my back. Confronted by the same thirty-two tiles, I was forced onto my left side, to face the door. I'd left it open. I wanted it closed. But damn it, I'd not get up. I wouldn't.

So I let it creak. The baby from next door howled at some point, with a drawn out keening kind of screech, one like

I'd never heard it make before, and I stuffed my fingers in my ears to shut out the sound of it and my own visceral response that had me wanting to fill my arms. The howling didn't stop abruptly, but dissipated like water down a drain.

My forearm muscles relaxed, letting the pillow ease back off my temples. Surely the mother has fed it or changed it and made everything right as rain. Perhaps it was even down for the night, if it was indeed night: I had no idea what time of day it was. It could easily be nine pm. I found myself listening hard for the shuffle of feet next door. I'd never thought before that perhaps my side of the apartment building was perfect for bedrooms. It was an old house, after all, turned into impromptu bachelor pads and low rentals for single moms. Bedrooms in old houses often crouched in the same parts, either facing the morning sun or hiding from it depending on the owner's preference.

No wonder so much of my days were marked by an infant's cry. It probably went down for naps as often as I was in my bedroom, maybe more. At least it did seem to be sleeping more and more lately in these last weeks; I heard it cry less often. Maybe it was growing out of the colic. Small blessings.

I listened again, this time out of curiosity. What did it look like now, this infant? Not quite so newborn as it was when I'd first glimpsed it, surely. Then I couldn't tell if it was a boy or a girl because its blanket was green: society's ironic notion of gender neutrality, their way of recognizing the zie of an unborn fetus. I wondered at that strange understanding that could lead a culture to provide gender neutral colors to expectant mothers, but shift so suddenly to a biased hue as soon as the baby is born. Thinking for some reason that the infant would prefer one to the other, that society needed to label a newborn person unable to do anything but pee and cry as one thing or another before the person could be asked. The notion was preposterous.

I listened harder. Nothing. It must be far into the

evening for there to be no sounds at all next door. Surely I'd hear some little thing. I stole a quick glance at the clock on my nightstand: six thirty. Morning, I wondered, or evening? I looked at the door to see how the light played on the room better, hoping to gauge the time of day. Nope. I could easily make out every detail. It couldn't be anywhere near night: dusk, maybe, but not nighttime. The clock must be right: 6:30 pm.

That meant there should be some movements next door. When you're moving around, doing your daily things, you're aware of the subtly of life around you without being thoroughly conscious of it: the fridge running, the murmur of voices in the apartment next to yours, the inevitable clanking of dishes that you just filter out as unimportant. When everything is silent, you are aware of the distinctness of each sound. The fridge could be running too fast, its motor about to burn out, or the murmur is angry, the clanking of dishes too sharp for you to bear.

There was nothing.

The question for me really was whether I cared enough to continue listening. What did it matter to me if the baby was napping or not? What should it matter? It shouldn't. And yet, knowing what was going on next door seemed the most important thing in the world to me. I closed my eyes again, willing the sound of my heartbeat to become audible, imagining the beads of color beneath my eyelids to become one blurred mess of black. It must have worked; sometime later, I thought my limbs grew heavy and the bedroom retreated like the pullout in a movie frame. I felt removed from existence in the sweet serenity of black out. Somewhere in the fog of it all, I could hear the low sound of muffled crying.

Chapter 6

I made every effort the next morning to call in sick. I willed myself to wake at a decent hour, I prepared my outfit mentally as I lay in bed, imagining the blouse I'd slip on, the sensible shoes that would match. I rehearsed my speech: "Yes, sir, you did hire a man three months ago, but if you look closely at the application, you'll see that I penciled in 'both' under gender, and now my spirit tells me I'm a woman. And isn't it illegal for you to ask a person that anyway?"

If I managed to get through that little intriguing episode, the other hurdles would certainly pose their own issues. The office supply store's back room was a hard job for anyone let alone a 165 pound woman whose muscles had been pummeled into bread dough. I knew I was too sore yet to lug boxes of paper and stock shelves, up the ladder, down the ladder. I was too sore yet to even move far past my bedroom to make the call.

I pressed one heated sole onto the cold laminate floor and pushed myself to a sitting position only to realize that all the toxins beaten from my muscles had taken up residence in the softer tissues beneath my joints. Every movement made me feel like I hadn't been oiled in months.

Instead of making the call, I fell back onto the pillow and resigned myself to taking cleansing breaths. A peek at the clock told me I'd overslept my alarm anyway. It was already 8:35 in the morning. I could understand oversleeping the alarm, but oversleeping the baby's hunger tantrums two days in a row? Not likely.

I lay there for several minutes letting the sounds of my apartment settle around me so I could more easily pick out the ones from the apartment next door. Surely the woman over there would draw a bath or rattle a pot or two. I didn't think she worked. I'd seen the baby once when we both stood at our mailboxes at the front door. It was not cute in the way newborns are a sort of vulnerable cute. It was peculiar looking, with a large head and limbs that seemed too small, too scrawny to be a thriving being. I remember it cried the whole time she jammed her key in the lock, but she didn't try to hush it or coo to it. I remember thinking I wanted the thing to shut up, or for her to at least make the effort to keep it quiet. The sounds of its squall sent bamboo shoots into the nails of my psyche.

Now I wondered how the woman could possibly have ignored her baby's distress so easily. Small details came to me now as I stretched carefully into the sheets. Despite the infant's peculiar look, it had the smallest, most perfectly shaped ears: like pink opaque teacups. I touched my own earlobe above where the stitches had begun to itch. There was a scab of blood there, I thought, and scratched at it till it came free. Yes, blood, a glob of dried brown that reminded me how fragile everything was. That baby. Was it flourishing? Did its mother love it?

I stayed like that, intermittently watching the ceiling, listening for sounds from next door, then falling asleep for hours. Listening for those sounds became an obsession while I was awake. I'd catch my hands beginning a trek to my cheek or my ribs and I'd force the hand to the wall, trying to will the sound waves from there to move up my skin. If it wasn't for the occasional muffled sob and rustle that could have been rats along the wall, I'd have thought that she'd just gone out. Taken the baby and gone shopping.

Molly phoned early in the afternoon, yanking me out of the weird reverie I'd let myself sink into.

"Jay? You busy. I need to come over."

"I'm tired, Mol."

"Tired," she echoed as though she'd never heard the word before. "You don't know tired. Look, I need to see you."

I thought about it; really, I did. I wasn't ready for her to see me.

"No, Mol. I just can't."

"Please."

I sighed. "I'm in bed."

"At three in the afternoon? You on crack?" It was a joke; I knew it was a joke, but I didn't find it funny.

"You know I'd never do that shit." My voice was hard, even I heard it.

She was all-apologetic. "I know; sheesh. Joking. You lost your sense of humor when you gave up the smack."

"I can't, Mol. Really. I'm just wagged."

There was a silence on the other end that sent a niggle down my spine, but I couldn't let it climb to the base of my neck and out my mouth. I forced myself to speak again before I could change my mind.

"I'm still mad at you."

"You'll get over it."

"No, I won't. I won't get over it. I don't want to see you." I knew it was mean. Still, I couldn't stop myself. I hung up then, and lay back against the pillows, watching the clock, listening pathetically for sounds from next door that never came.

By the time the clock shifted to 6:27 pm, I began to believe something was wrong.

I told myself I was being foolish, but I couldn't shake the intuition that sat on me with a dread as sure as death. I'd wait another few hours, though. Just to be sure. Maybe two. And then what?

I couldn't exactly demand to be let in, and even if I did manage to get my hard-looking old self over there, what would I say was the reason I was calling? I had no real cause to call 911. Maybe I'd wait till tomorrow and hope to see her at the mailbox again. I began to fantasize about it, seeing bright eyes peeking over a blanket, hearing a coo as the mother stuck her finger in its grip, smelling that smell that followed babies everywhere, of soap and milk and powder.

Two thirty of the next afternoon came, and still no shrill cries. Supper came and went with me lying in nearly the same position I'd started in but for a few sortings and re-sortings of my limbs in between the hours. I got up late in the evening feeling a bit more capable of moving my body and less inclined to move my spirit. I foraged in the cupboards for a snack and came away with three bags of microwave popcorn in a lite, 100 calorie flavor. I bubbled up a half cup of butter and poured it over the top. I pulled a Pepsi from the fridge and eased myself onto the couch, shoveling handfuls into my mouth and letting sips of cola erode the puffs. The television, black and silent, stared back at me.

Once I thought I heard a door slam in the next apartment, and my chest tripped over itself trying to keep my heart calm. So. Someone was home.

Two days went like that as though they were two hours. I'm not sure where the individual moments went as I lay in bed or sat in my chair staring at CBC. At one point, I remember seeing the remote sitting on top of the television but I couldn't see any reason to get up and retrieve it to switch channels. I'm sure I was aware of things as each moment passed: a need to urinate, a growl in my stomach that signaled a need for food, the flickerings of *The Hour* and *Air Farce* and *Rick Mercer*, but when the moments were over, I couldn't mark any one of them with any specificity. I just knew that by the time these days were done, I was able to wash my face without too much pain. My face seemed more angular on the right side rather than the puffy and swollen thing it had been; the bruises began to turn green and yellow around the edges, and the stitches itched as the skin pulled tighter in its knit.

And yet, despite the passing of these apathetic hours, once or twice I caught myself in a tense posture, the muscles in my thighs tight and poised, my head cocked slightly to the side. I was ready. Waiting. Fight or flight, I wasn't sure, but I was ready. I just had no idea what I was ready for until I found myself standing on my bed with a glass against my bedroom wall, my ear pressed to it, straining for the sound of crying and hearing nothing that remotely sounded like a baby.

It was peculiar, this focus I had on something that wasn't happening, that I wasn't hearing. After all the drugs, self-mutilation, and sex that had failed to bring some sense of life to this shell of a body, I could hardly believe that the lack of infant crying could jumpstart something within me that resembled some sort of empathy. I wasn't sure how to feel about the spark firing up again; I'd spent so much time making sure it was extinguished, the dead tiredness of explaining myself to everyone. Out of habit, I tried to tamp it down now. I tried to ignore it, and find within that comfortable blanket of complacency that would let me continue to survive, if not thrive. That had been good enough all these years, hadn't it?

I did make an effort to call into work on the third morning and got yelled at by the supervisor who took my call. With a relief I didn't understand, I pressed the green button that clipped off the signal of my cell phone. I stared at the phone for some time. So. That was that. I was remotely surprised that I felt no remorse at losing a job for the first time in my life because of slackness rather than a sudden change of gender, and as I was considering how a person could so thoroughly screw themselves over financially and not care, I heard a loud slam from next door. The front door?

Not sure, I hurried to the window that afforded me a view of the porch that adjoined our apartments. No one there. I cocked my head, listening. Muffled sounds. Talking? Not to anyone, surely; there was no second voice and no shrill cries either. The laughter that came on the heels of a short one-sided conversation sounded manic. High pitched. Unnerving.

That was it. I just couldn't sit here in this apartment one more minute. It didn't matter what was going on or not going on over there, it was time I stepped back into reality. If that meant being neighborly, then to Hell with it. I'd be neighborly.

I ran for the cupboard and grabbed a grubby, plastic theatre cup with a Harry Potter, Hermione, and Ron collage. I needed sugar. Baking brownies. Yeah. Made perfect sense.

The next-door apartment's front door had scrapes down at the bottom as though a dog had nailed its insistent want for entrance over a dozen years. The mailbox was jammed with flyers and junk mail, coming out from beneath the black tin lid and threatening to fall to the floor. A ragged twenty-dollar stroller leant into the corner, its three wheels caked in muck that had long dried but not fallen onto the floor.

I rapped smartly before I could lose my nerve. I expected the sporadic titters inside to stop and for the person to come to the door. No one came. The manic laughter stopped to be replaced by a muttering that I thought sounded pretty much like, "Fuck you. Go to Hell," and a few other statements that were less discernable, but no less curse-riddled.

I rapped again. "Are you okay in there?"

I could swear I heard her tell me to fuck off again. "Come on; I'm from next door. I'm worried about you. Are you okay?"

I rattled the doorknob and regret tripped through my chest when I felt the knob turn all the way to the left. A quick, breath-catching slap of fear struck as the sound of thundering footsteps from within charged toward me and the open door. The door sucked itself open, pulling a draft of air from the porch inwards and past me. Shit. Too late. I was committed.

The face that met me would have been beautiful if it visaged a woman in her right mind. The proportions were perfect, youthful if you looked past the pitted teeth. I got the feeling she might be intelligent; her gaze was shrewd, even if it had the drugged look of a crack addict.

"You've got no business here." Her face had a pinched, tight look. The pupils pulled themselves in like black holes, nearly disappearing for the greed of light that might escape.

I proffered my grubby cup. What I planned to come out nice and smooth came out in a stammer. "I thought I'd borrow some sugar..." It sounded horribly stupid once it came out, and I knew she didn't believe me.

She smirked at me and brushed a lank, filthy bit of hair off her forehead. It would be pretty washed, that hair. Auburn, the shade would be, not this ratty, oily brown.

I jumped onto another precarious limb, thinking a shot at honesty might wipe the scowl from her face. "That's not true, that bit about needing sugar," I said. "I just made that up."

"No shit," she said and started to close the door. Her arms were scrawny and the skin shadowed along the muscle line looked gray. I stuck out my hand and gripped her forearm, what was there of it, at least. She felt as scrawny as she looked. I found myself desperately wishing for that apathy to settle round my shoulders again.

"Really. I'm worried."

"Worry about someone who cares."

At this, she pushed at the door and I had to withdraw my hand. I went back to my apartment feeling like a failure. The shrill pleading of the phone had me rushing into my apartment and down the hall. I was out of breath and feeling as though I'd regressed a few days in my recovery by the time I answered it.

"How come you're out of breath?"

My mother. "No reason," I said.

"Were you running or something?"

"Well, for the phone, obviously."

"Maybe you should get more exercise then."

"I'm in plenty good shape."

"If you're that out of breath grabbing for the phone, you have problems. Have you been to the doctor lately?"

Had I? I wanted to laugh except I knew where this was really going. She worried about the A disease like most people worried about cancer. "I'm fine."

"I haven't seen any drunken pictures on Facebook lately." It was an accusation on two counts: she hadn't been able to keep tabs on me even peripherally, and if she had been able to, she would disapprove of what she thought were drunks. No winning on that one.

"I haven't been out." It was too close to the truth so I changed the subject the best way I knew: talk about her. "Have you been keeping busy?"

The strategy worked. She erupted in a lengthy diatribe of the comings, goings, and dramas of the 'Drama Society,' an elitist group that kept odd company with each other in ways that made the LGBT community seem frivolous. I'd often told her that kind of upper crust was far too crusty for her. It was a veritable soap opera within the society, no pun intended. Not that she had any problems with gossip; it was the other stuff she'd abhor: the stuffiness, the holier than thous, Apparently, this time she'd been accused of trying to choke another actor over his comments during their highbrow discussion of her interpretation of a particular line. This latter part of the conversation actually got my attention, knowing my mother as I did.

"Did he press charges?"

"What charges?" The level and tone of her voice didn't change; it had the same intensity and level of indignance as when she'd recounted the accusation. "He was perfectly fine the whole time; I just reached out to fix his tie for him."

I knew the man she spoke of; he was a hot-blooded Acadian fisherman who fancied his career on the water had all been an insufferable bit of happenstance. If he wore a tie, he was going to a funeral. "So," I said again. "Did he press charges?"

There was dead air for a short spell and then she came back with: "He eventually agreed that there was no reason to involve the police." She said this with extreme dignity, which led me to believe she'd used the tone on him to satisfying effect.

I had a quick image from my childhood of her throwing a pot of drained but saucy spaghetti noodles at my father because he'd been out half an hour past supper and smelled of perfume and tobacco. She'd never had a great deal of restraint when she lost her temper. I didn't know what to say; I imagined her attempt to strangle the man came and went as quickly as the heat of a hand laid on a hot surface: repealed quickly but lingering long after.

She must have noted my silence and figured I understood completely because she abruptly changed the subject. "I've made your favorite for supper. You want to come out?"

"I've never liked lasagna."

"What makes you think it's lasagna, Robert?"

"It's J, Mom."

"Jay?" she said. "What's Jay? Some sort of poultry dish?" she had an infuriating way of pretending ignorance when confronted with something she didn't like. I chewed a bit of skin off the inside of my mouth.

"You know what J is."

"Not that again."

"Yes, that. Again."

"I don't want to argue. I just wanted you to come for supper. I haven't seen you in ages."

"I was over last weekend."

"You used to enjoy being home."

I thought about that. There was a time when I spent a lot of time there; not so much secure in the fact that I wouldn't have to pretend to be something I wasn't, but because it was far too exhausting to pretend with strangers than with family. To her, it might have seemed as though I felt comfortable there. I wondered about that, and ended up feeling as though pieces of my psyche were falling away. I could scrabble for them, surely, piece them together like a jigsaw.

"Well?" she prodded.

"Sure, Mum, I'll come," I said hastily, then: "I'll come." This time less certain, regretful.

"Great. I made a nice lasagna."

I hung up feeling as though I'd gone through the rabbit hole. What was I thinking to agree to visit looking like I did? My stomach twittered and I got up to look for some antacid to coat the nerves that had begun to fire down there. Because I was rummaging through the medicine cabinet, I almost missed the sound of rapping on my door. It was only the insistent pounding it became that drew my attention away from the dark recesses of six square inches of hemorrhoid cream and massage oils.

She looked just as mad, just as distraught, and just as high as when I'd first gone over a mere ten minutes before.

"Come on in." I opened the door, noticing that she had brought along a small plastic container--the excuse should she need it.

She noticed me looking and shuffled it behind her back awkwardly. I heard a dull thunk through the fake cough she made as she dropped it behind her.

I swept my arm across the open expanse of space the door made as I opened it. "I'm glad you're here."

She looked back over her shoulder but eased into my apartment the way a thief might except she looked directly at me, wary almost, but direct. "I'm sorry," she said.

"S'okay."

I stood there in the hall, the door still open, my hand on the edge of it, not sure if I should close it or hold it for her so she could bolt.

"I wanted--"

"You wanted me to mind my business, I know."

"No, it's just that--"

"Just that I have no right to interfere."

"Shut up," she said and the pupils that wouldn't dilate in the gloom of the hall seemed to spark strangely. Must have been my imagination. "You keep interrupting."

You can imagine that I literally had to clamp my lips down at that; instead, I ushered her in and closed the door. I snapped on the hall light, thinking it would make my apartment seem more welcoming. She flinched.

"It's okay," I said and turned it back off.

She waved a weak hand in the air but said nothing.

"You want to come in?" I beckoned toward the living room, a small compartment with a decent looking couch I'd found on the side of the road during Spring Cleanup and had sent out for cleaning. The cheap '80s lamp in the corner glowed on its first of three settings. It looked decidedly cozy in there.

She nodded quietly and slipped off her flipflops. We looked at each other for a few long moments, each of us, I suppose, feeling like old dogs that didn't have the ability to circle their beds before settling in. Finally, she broke the silence.

"You look like I feel."

I touched my face absently, feeling the roughness of the stitches. I'd forgotten how I might look; I'd been avoiding the mirror except for the initial morning check to see if I was progressing in my healing.

"Pretty recent, huh?" she asked.

I nodded, still not sure whether I should say anything or not and she made a sort of groan that could have been displeasure or mourning. "Fuckers," she said and I got the feeling her vehemence had nothing to do with my fading bruises.

I waited as she sat down gingerly on the edge of the farthest cushion. "I figured looking like that you might actually..." she trailed off and I waited as long as I could before I had to prod her.

"Actually?"

She fell back staring at the ceiling. Her movements were lazy as she waved her hand around but there was something coiled within her core that kept her back rigid. "I don't know how to say it."

"Just say what you think."

"Oh, to Hell with it." She jerked off the couch and fled back toward the hall.

"Fuckers beat me to within an inch of death," I said now that she was here, now that I had within my grasp the answer to the weird feelings I'd had over the strange lack of infant crying, I wasn't about to let her go.

It could have been true. Fact is, everyone loves a bit of juicy gossip. I hated using the F word; it always felt so filthy, but the fact that she'd used it made it the most sensible thing to slip in to get her attention. It succeeded. She belted round. She stood at the edge of the living room a mere foot or so from the hall, holding that tense posture of a rabbit before it bolts.

She swayed a bit to the left. "Who was it?"

I shrugged.

Her gaze went to my ear. "You went to the hospital." It was a statement, not meant to get more out of me, just to show she was observant enough to notice the stitches, which in turn meant she believed the part about an inch of death.

"Twelve of them," I said of the stitches. "Three days ago."

"Shit," she exclaimed and moved back into the room to investigate my face more thoroughly. I felt peculiar, as though I was a 1800s African slave being inspected by a driver, but I forced myself to endure her prodding gaze, uncomfortable as it was. "That's pretty nasty looking to be only three days old."

Again, I shrugged. I only had previous beatings to compare to. They all seemed to take forever to heal. Two eternities to forget. "I have a big mouth. Gets me into trouble."

"You file charges?"

"On who?" I asked. "Never saw them before."

She screwed her eyes into a narrowed gaze of iris-filled

space. The pinpoints of pupils refused to play with the color. "It's happened before?"

"It always happens."

"I know," she said and promptly clamped her mouth shut.

"It's okay," I reassured her. "I get it."

"It's not like it's happened to me or anything."

"Of course not."

"It's just the stupid luck of it all. Shit always happens. You know?"

"I know," I said, letting her feel as though I completely understood.

She looked round the living room. "My kitchen's here. Opposite of what your apartment is."

I followed her gaze to where the bathroom would be. "I bet the rest is the same though," I said.

She nodded. "Two bedrooms."

"I use one as a storage room," I told her, thinking she'd imagine cartons and boxes and filing cabinets. Whether or not I wanted it to, an image of the spare room, filled with feather boas and masculine ties in a jumbled mess, came to mind.

I took a few timid steps toward her and extended my hand. Despite the intent, I was still surprised when she took it and followed me to the couch. She settled in. Her hands began to pleat her pajama pants above the knee where her legs must have slimmed out considerably; there was barely any leg thickness beneath the fabric in contrast to a rather wide hip. I scanned her face and neck for the certain signs of bulimia or anorexia. Grayish look to her skin, muscles standing out but mere bits of cord around her bones, teeth yellowed. Sure enough signs. In light of the pupils, however, I doubted she had an eating disorder.

"How's the baby?" I blurted and could have bitten the end of my tongue off and happily chewed on it when I saw the look come across her face. I expected, in light of the frantic expression, for her to jump off the sofa again and swear at me, running to the door. Because she stayed put, in exactly the same position, I guessed she was weighing out whether she should talk to me.

I leaned back, trying to look as though I didn't really want to know, or at the very least, didn't feel as though it mattered. It was hard trying not to show that I'd been listening at the baby's bedroom wall for nearly three days. I caught myself peeling bits of frayed skin off my bottom lip with my teeth.

Finally, she took a deep breath like she was about to dive into the waves at our frigid water beach. "She's gone," she said. "They took her."

"Took her?"

Her head waggled up and down and with each bob she gripped her knees tighter with spidery fingers. Her face remained impassive. A stray lock of dirty hair fell in front of her left eye and she didn't bother to move it aside.

"Who took her?"

She shrugged but the movement was spare. Her lips were tight.

"Is she in danger?"

This time, she did bolt, startling me enough to jump off my perch and follow her to the kitchen where she'd undoubtedly mis-aimed her feet in her haste to get out and missed the hall by a long shot. I caught her by the fridge door.

"My oven is here," she said, sweeping an arm across the appliance. I wanted to throttle Vanna White in the instant for showing a million viewers such an expansive movement that could encompass everything and yet nothing at all. "On the opposite wall."

She spun in a slow circle, running her hand across the wall for as long as she could, then wrapped it around her waist when the wall ran out.

"Yeah, your apartment is very much like mine. Just in reverse." She squeezed her ribcage with her arms. Hugging herself. I wanted to step forward and pull her into a real embrace.

I was about to say her name but realized I didn't know it. Why was I bothering again? For someone I didn't know?

"You said someone took the baby." I pressed on.

"Yup." It was a matter of fact answer, followed up with a frenetic nod as though I couldn't somehow understand English all of a sudden. I had to jam the tip of an impatient tongue into the roof of my mouth for an instant or two before speaking again.

"And...?"

She headed to the hall, aiming her feet with deliberation this time. "And nothing. Just she's gone, is all."

I had to project my voice ahead of me as I followed her the short distance to the door, hoping I could stop her. "Wait."

She twirled around, lifting an over-plucked brow in query.

I cast around my vacuous head for a staller and came up with an equally good a one as my original excuse of needing to borrow sugar.

"I ordered a pizza to come at five. Way too big for one person. Figured I'd eat it for a couple days instead of cooking, but you could have some."

"Ok," she said and there was a peculiar hungry look to her expression that belied the nonchalance of her answer. "Why not?"

"Yeah. Why not?" I said, not expecting the answer to be positive; I'd only thought about as far as keeping her from leaving. There was no pizza.

"Great," I said. "Um. Why not have a seat. I'll just phone up. Make sure they still have the order." Stupid, I know, but what would you do?

I took my time getting to my bedroom where an old rotary phone sat on my bureau. I'd picked it up at a yard sale for a dime when I'd returned home and figured it would be great for those times when the power went out, as it's wont to do in rural Nova Scotia in the dead of January.

I ordered the pizza and told them to bring it straight away.

"I asked them to put lots of meat and cheese on," I said to her when I came back out into the living room. "Turns out I'm pretty hungry. You?"

She nodded hastily. "I could eat a horse."

"And chase the rider?"

She tittered; maybe feeling more light hearted knowing she'd be eating soon. "I'd leave the saddle, though," she said. "Too tough."

I smiled for her as much and as genuinely as I could with the crackling of my stitches filling my ear. "I'm J."

She stuck her hand out. "Stephanie."

The formality threw me for a second but I managed to step forward and thrust my palm into hers. It was moist and cool. A limp pump.

"Nice to meet you Stephanie."

Oddly enough, it was this stiff formality that took the biggest toll. She collapsed onto the floor like a crumpled paper bag blown too big and popped. It took me a few seconds to register that she'd fallen.

"Are...are you okay?" I watched her pull her legs into the lotus position. Pretty flexible, for a filthy urchin. She leaned over them, weaving up and down as though she was crying, but no sound came out at all. Not even a moan or a simper. I had the feeling this posture had been settled into pretty often as of late. I wasn't sure what to do.

"Stephanie?"

I tried to ease closer, feeling about as useful as a ballerina with rubber boots. "Stephanie, I can help."

I heard an odd sound of laugher bubble beneath her chest; it sounded bitter and angry. Despite the bells sounding in my head that told me that the bell was tolling for no one in the near vicinity and I should mind my own damn business, I forged ahead. My curiosity, you see. It's always been my downfall. And the baby. I really wanted to know. No. I had to know.

"I can help. Really."

She looked up at me from her spot on the carpet. Her face blanched, her eyes wild looking. "Yeah. You think?"

"Well. Yeah. Sure. Why not?"

"You got no idea."

I was pretty sure she was right and that I had absolutely no idea, but I'd gone too far now to stop. "Try me."

She sighed at that, almost an exaggerated sense of impatience. "They took her."

"They?"

"Yeah. They."

I waited for her to expound on the pronoun. It seemed I'd have to wait several minutes while she stared at me, staring me down, daring me it seemed. I worked to keep my body language as quiet as my lips, but my mind was racing, spilling over with nagging wants to push her further. It was a real struggle to focus.

"They," she said finally, "are Social Services."

"Ah," I said. And it dawned on me. I couldn't help her at all.

Chapter 7

Ten minutes into Stephanie's tirade of how the bastards had taken her baby girl and how they didn't care that she had been clean for the last six months of her pregnancy, how she stayed clean for at least two weeks of the baby's life and that was damned hard, it was and I thought I was going to tear my hair out. Still it didn't stop. How dare they come and just take her like that when she'd worked so hard for that baby. Gave up the junk. Kept the baby clean. Fed her. Put her to bed and let her cry herself to sleep so she wouldn't get spoiled, my God, we couldn't have that, could we because then what were the poor thing's chances then if she got picked up and cuddled every time she whimpered. She, so delicate, so small that it was tough to pull her sleepers down over her head without scratching skin with fingernails, hard to manage to dress the little thing without making her cry. God. Did those bastards have any idea how hard it was to live a life with a thing so small?

Ah yes, ten minutes of this and I realized I'd missed supper at my mom's and knew I'd have to pay for it later when she'd finally call, all fitted up with fury.

But what could I do except keep listening? I passed over a piece of pizza, cold by now from sitting in its open box on the upended lobster crate I used as a coffee table. She reached out to take what I left, her fourth piece, and jammed it into her mouth as though it was her first. I used the silence of her chewing to ask the question I'd been begging to ask since the soliloquy had begun.

"Exactly what did they say when they took her?"

She shrugged and spoke through a full mouth. "Failure to thrive."

"What the Hell does that mean?"

"Don't ask me, some stupid excuse to take a baby away from its mother, is all I know. Bastards. One of them--fucken cow-- had the nerve to stick her finger onto the table and swipe across it like I was some kind of filthy housekeeper or something. Said my house--my house," she yelled this as she repeated it and stabbed her chest with the hand holding the pizza, letting some sauce drip onto my couch, "was not conducive to a baby's healthy living."

"Conducive? Pretty hoity toity word."

"Ya think?" She muttered, "Bitch," under her breath. "But that's what she said. Said it like I wouldn't know what it meant." Stephanie studied the crust on the pizza slice. "She needs to have something swiped across her throat if you ask me."

"So did you try to find out what failure to thrive means?"

She stared at me. "What difference does it make? Nothing makes a difference. They been waiting for me to screw up. Knew I would." She looked down into her lap and I thought I heard her choke on the bit of pizza she had in her mouth until she spoke again, seconds later, as though I wasn't there. "They knew I would. Bastards."

The way she said it, so defeated, made me want to pull her into an embrace, make it better, shoo away the boogey man.

"Listen, I don't know what your history is, but they can't possibly know..." Even as I said it, she looked straight at me, her pupils beginning to adjust and readjust in the light, fidgety like she'd grown in the last few minutes, and I knew. "It's happened before."

"It always happens."

"Always?"

She nodded. "Happened to my sister and her baby, happened to my first baby. They took him when he was a month old. I was only fifteen. I didn't know any better." She got up and started to pace, the trips she took back and forth dizzying in the speed of 180s. "But I know now. I wanted this baby. I wanted to care for her. I wanted to show them I could do it this time. I'm a good mom. A real good mom. My house might not be a showcase, but the baby, she's clean. She's fed. You gotta believe me."

I wanted to believe her. It was just the frenetic nature of her confession that lent me doubts. Her intent might have been pure, but her practice surely was not or they'd not have taken the baby. Perhaps she wasn't capable of being a good mother. I watched her as she looked at me. Her ribcage trembled, and the sweater she was wearing, full of muddy stains, made me imagine her apartment, the finger that swept across a table. Had there just been dust on that table or had the coating been full of various types of powders that congeal in the air from nefarious smokes and fall in particles? I wondered what the social worker had seen. I thought of what the sideboards must look like: full of dirty pots, opened condiment jars, stacks of dishes. Blackened glass tubes. I thought of the baby and the way it looked perfectly formed, but just not 'right' somehow.

I thought of all this, and I couldn't imagine myself telling her I believed her. The most I could imagine was trying to help her now. And even that, I knew from experience was something I couldn't do without enabling her habits. I couldn't help her without getting enmeshed. And I didn't need that. I had enough on my plate. I had to deal with my own shit.

My silence must have made her uncomfortable. She'd started scanning the room and the fidgeting she'd begun during her last bit of pizza had worked its way into a passion. I got the feeling she was fighting off the need to leave.

"Does it hurt much?" she asked.

"Hurt?"

She nodded. "Your face."

"Oh," I said. To be honest, I'd not given it any thought in the hours. "Only when I think about it."

Her hand crept up beneath the hair at the back of her neck and kneaded the muscles there. "That's good. That's good," she said, but her tone was distracted. She wasn't looking at me.

"Yeah," I said. "It is."

"Cause, you know, I could..."

I lifted a brow in query and she halted mid-sentence, gave a squeeze to her shoulder as she let her hand fall. "I could. I just thought--"

"Thought?"

"Well, you know. I have something can help that."

My stomach made a gurgling sound that had nothing to do with digestion of the few slices of pizza. My cheeks sent a sudden splash of water into my mouth. I forced words into the flood, hoping the instantaneous response would dry up the familiar and unwanted want of what she was offering.

"No. No, it's okay."

"Are you sure? I have--well, not plenty--but I have some. Enough."

I shook my head. "I can't." Was all I could manage around the tightening of my cheeks.

She nodded slowly and with careful deliberation, trod her way to the hallway. I followed her out and closed the door behind her.

She was gone. I knew what she'd be doing in that apartment of hers, maybe not the minute details, but I knew the general idea. Shuffling her pain to the back of her psyche, that's what she'd be doing. Driving it away with counterfeit willpower.

I touched my cheek far below the tenderness of the wound there. It still hurt too much to touch directly. Even the flesh of my cheekbone ached when my fingers probed around. Closer I got to the stitches and cakieness of the cut, the more it hurt. I thought of the reason I had that injury. I thought of the self-inflicted pains and the remedies prescribed from a self that had no idea how to soothe or salve and chose instead the harsher medicines. The proverbial disreputable narcotic when an over-the-counter cough tonic would do. I thought of how badly, for the first time in over one year and six days and three hours, that I wanted to dull the pain.

My fingers went to the closest stitch of their own volition. The second they touched, the bit of synthetic cat gut sent a warning down the tremors of my jaw line. I thought of the first boy who'd called me a name: freak. I closed my eyes with the pain of the memory. His mother had brought him over to my house on a playdate. I'd decided to put on my mom's high heels, thinking more of the word date than play. I remembered his face, the way he screwed up his mouth in disgust. There was a sense of a stomachache that didn't feel right. It ached all the way up to my throat, and I felt as though I'd peed myself in front of someone.

On the heels of that memory came the mouth-drying smack of need. I felt as though my legs were trembling with their want to run.

My fingers tightened around the stitch. I pulled gently at first, an experimental movement that did indeed demonstrate how sore the injury still was. I reveled in the sense of it, that pain, reminding me how good it was to feel. I thought of how perfectly and completely heroin always sucked any kind of feeling away. How it left me deliriously vacuous. Empty. Dull.

Still, it was meth that got me. Left me euphoric, energized, ready to take on the world and beat it to a bloody pulp if need be. Heroin had been beautifully emptying, but meth gave me balls. Woe to the bully who took me on, on meth. I was a wild thing. I carried a knife. I wanted to use it. Too often, I used it on myself when the energy ran out, when I was left like a rag on my bed too tired from tweaking to do much but remember that boy and his twisted mouth: all the twisted mouths I'd seen.

I closed my eyes with the remembrance of all of it, determined, and pulled as hard as I dared on the stitch between my fingers.

It was only the sharpness of the hurt that made me realize how exhausted I was. I felt my way along the hall, my palms running along the *crepiness* of old wallpaper until finally I was at the living room. I swiped at a trickle that lent a flush of warmth to a narrow strip of neck, wiped it on my jeans without looking. I didn't need to see the blood to know I'd set the wound to running. Reopened wounds always ran.

I fell back onto the sofa, arms flung backwards over my head and dangling from the armrest. You have to know, I hadn't used in a very long time: in addict-time, even a day is an eternity. You have to know that I walked out of my rehabilitation committed to sobriety. You have to know too that no addict is ever safe. I knew I had dodged a bullet, to use the old cliché, but I also knew the distance between safety and snowed is microns thin.

She was next door. She had junk. I was lying around in my own misery. If ever there was a formula that could square a circle, this was it. Exhausted as I was, I'd have to keep my mind occupied. Otherwise, I'd chew that bit of information over in my mind like a piece of tobacco until the nicotine wore off and the ants under my skin went scuttling in search of a picnic.

As much as I'd want to avoid it, I knew I'd have to phone my mother; it would save me her anger at my unexcused absence from supper, and it would serve as a distraction. Better yet, I could go over, get away from the apartment and the knowledge that Stephanie was over there right now, either blowing smoke from a glass pipe or plunging a needle into her arm. I wondered which it was. The best of times was often the worst of times for me and meth, which was why I'd moved onto heroin when I got to the city. It calmed me.

If I had to call it, though, I'd have my doubts on Stephanie and meth. She had the hungry twitch of someone in the middle of a tweak--you know, fidgety, *talkity*, pronounced and dramatic moves, but if you've ever been around someone in the middle of a no sleep run, you'd notice the irritation and short fuse above all else. She was too clear headed for that, too maudlin, almost. I had my doubts about heroin either. Probably good old-fashioned Dilaudid or Ativan.

Just realizing I was running down a catalogue of possible legals and illegals made me realize how close I was to wanting to know exactly what she was using, and that meant a short hundred-yard dash to using myself. It drove me to my cellphone. I needed out and I knew it. Thank God Mum answered on the second ring.

"I'm coming over."

"Robert? Is that you?"

"You know who it is, Mum."

"You missed supper."

"I know. Company came over."

"It's nearly seven."

"I know."

"I go to my book club at 8."

I sighed. "I need to come over, Mum."

There was a pause on the other end, one that sent its message straight through the wires even before she spoke. "You're not on the dope again, are you, Robert? Cause if you are, I'm not giving you any money."

"It's J."

"Are you?"

"Yes." I heard the irritation in my voice, and though I knew it came from desperation, I also knew Mum wouldn't know that. I was about to apologize when she cut in.

"I knew it. Well, at least you have the decency not to lie this time. Do you need me to call 911?"

"What? 911? What for?"

"For you and the dope."

"I told you, I'm not on crank, Mum."

"You did so say so. You said yes."

"What? No. I said yes I was J; not yes I'm on the goddamned dope again."

There was a moment of silence between us before she spoke again--her tone filled with concern. "When are you coming? I can feign a headache and not go to my meeting."

It almost took me off guard. What was I thinking? I couldn't spend an evening there. I'd come straight home from Mom's and pound on Stephanie's door and my honorable escape would all be for naught. I inhaled slowly through my nose so my lungs filled. I could do this. I was a big boy. A big girl. A big whatever the Hell I was; I was too distraught to make the distinctions at the moment.

"Never mind, Mum. Go to your meeting. I'm fine."

"Are you sure?"

"Yeah."

"Robert?"

I didn't have the energy to argue. "Yeah," I said.

"Go to a meeting," she said.

"Yeah, that's probably the best idea."

"It's the only idea."

I hung up sensing that even though I felt as wrung out as an early morning face cloth, that at least she'd given me some decent advice. A meeting. I hadn't been to one since I stopped using. I'd beaten the dope and managed to stay clean without succumbing to the ever-threatening relapse and rehab cycle, not even once, and so what good was a meeting to me when I was this clean?

I pumped up my laptop and Googled Narcotics Anonymous in Nova Scotia, found my town's chapter and discovered the meetings were every Friday at 8 pm. Fat lot of good Friday did me; today was Wednesday. I tapped my nails against the side of the computer. The whole day had been one exhausting, grievant mess of hours.

I looked up the term Stephanie had mentioned. Failure to thrive was easy in definition it seemed, but difficult in diagnosis. In a nutshell, it meant the child had been unable to grow during an adequate amount of time. There was no real clear-cut definition, no clear-cut reason. Speculation included just about everything from neglect to lack of affection. I thought of Stephanie as I read, and I thought of her baby. I wondered about the term: thrive. My playdate's face came unbidden to my mind, and I squashed the image. You shall not thrive, I told it.

I fiddled around on Facebook for a while, creeping through profiles of people I knew in the city to see what they'd been up to while I was gone. Seems Cinnamon had made an appointment for her boobs, finally. Cinnamon was not a tranny; she was a full-blooded, wide-hipped beauty who had double A cups and a penchant for athletic women who liked large breasts. I clicked on 'like' but fell short of actually communicating with anyone. I wasn't ready. Too many of those people I knew were battling the same demons I had and I got away because I started to feel as though I was losing. If I gave in and started to chat with any of them, I as good as sealed my doom.

I went through a ravenous de-friend frenzy and when I was done, I crept over to Molly's page. She was still listed as: sitting on the dock of the bay: her idea of letting some friends know she was at the old family homestead while leaving mere acquaintances with no certainty her city apartment was empty. She thought it fooled the would-be robbers in the area where she lived. Ignoring that she'd been broken into one night while she slept the sleep of the drugged.

There were pictures of her posted from the night we were out: she'd made it into some redhead's panties, apparently, but the girl was not cute. Her nose was flat and wide and she was pulling the Hef scarf between her legs in a grotesque striptease act. Molly's gaze was distorted the way a photo is when it's taken from an arm's length, and it stared out from the Internet in a way that suggested, "See, J? I absolutely can get laid looking like this."

Well, bully for her. I wondered how that girl felt the

next morning, knowing she'd been queered in.

I clicked a few more photos, and sure enough, in the background of one I could see an out of focus baggie. I tried to make the picture bigger so I could see what was in the bag.

We'd spent a good many mornings together, Molly and I, because we'd spent a good many late nights together. I knew her after-morning drug choice: coke. Enough, actually, over the last few times that I'd begun to wonder if Molly's queer skin had grown too tight for the sanctimonious beast within. I wondered how she could still be going. I'd have been dead by now. Had come close enough that last time that I could tell the reaper's cloak was made of soft, come-hither velvet and not cold satin.

Yes, it had been close. And intentional. Some addicts end up doing themselves in because they know their addiction is one they can't kick, and they know equally as well that they can't live with the shame of letting the monkey crap down their neck daily. Some addicts do it accidentally a little too much after an agonizing dry spell, a bit of unrefined shit, too refined shit, or just shit in disguise.

Us transgendered folk? Hell, we know how to throw a pity party, invite the neighbors and act as a piñata.

So, I had a double dose of intentional. I couldn't imagine that Molly was still doing all that, but I knew she had to find her own bottom and claw her own way through the roots and rocks to the top. Shit. Over a year since I'd made my final decision, and she was still grabbing for that dragon's tail?

I felt a frantic urge to shut the computer off before I could see any more. I pressed the power bar with my foot.

Chapter 8

My feet were under me and on the floor before I could think about it. I had the feeling I was pulling off a Band-Aid: get going, get over there, get in there before I could think about it too much. It was almost surreal. Even the four smart raps on Stephanie's door seemed out of focus. She didn't answer. I twisted the knob. It gave way and the door swung open like it had earlier in the afternoon.

"Stephanie?" I fairly jumped inside and closed the door with a soft click. "Hey. You in here?"

I heard a short movement as though someone had rolled off something onto the floor. The voice that came was stupefied. "Down here."

I didn't bother with my shoes, just scurried to the living room.

She was indeed on the floor, legs splayed in front of her, back against the couch. She wore a lopsided smile that looked limp enough that I could lay bets on the surety of drool on her chin.

"You okay?"

She squealed with forced laughter. "I'm right as rain as my mom would say." She stretched out the last word with a slur and looked up at me, her neck a weak pillar for her head. "Isn't that a stupid thing to say?"

"What did you take?"

She shrugged with her left shoulder; the other one just sort of drooped there and ended with her hand on the carpet.

"Stephanie?"

She burbled.

"Stephanie, I need to know what you've taken." I leaned in, closer, close enough that when her gaze met mine, I could almost make out my reflection in the glassiness of her stare. When she didn't answer, I took a quick scan of the room. Shit, no. Please tell me I wasn't going to have to deal with a manic overdose. I didn't have the heart today.

"Stephanie," I said again slowly, pronouncing each syllable, and she burbled again. "Where's your stash?"

Her face lit up. "You want some? I got some." She made an attempt to stand but fell onto her side, laughing. "Shit. I've fallen and I can't get up." She squealed again and lay down, her cheek on her bicep. "You get it, J."

My cheeks felt as though I'd bitten into a lemon. "You tell me where it is and I'll get it."

She waved the free arm over her head and waggled it toward the corner where a milk crate harbored an armful of stuffed toys.

"It's in the toy box?"

She nodded. "Best hiding place ever."

I made my way over, dreading that the stash would actually be there. She wouldn't be so dumb, would she? I peeked in, trying to see whether there was a plastic baggie, a glass vial, anything, and her voice came from behind me, stealing my attention but not relieving the nagging climb of nerves up my back.

"You gotta dig. It's at the bottom. The battery compartment. Got that at Frenchy's. Baby never got to play with it, though. Never got to."

I dug around, fishing through cheap dollar store toys and ratty stuffed animals. "Never got to play with what? Battery compartment of what, Stephanie? What?"

She sucked her teeth. "You dummy. The Crybaby doll." She started to sing rock-a-bye-baby and I thought I was going to lose my mind with the off-rhythm, off-canting of it. It was like listening to tomcats trying to mewl Carmen.

When my hand touched a plush thing with a hard, square center, I couldn't help whooping. "Got it." I took it out and brandished it, victorious. "Got it." I showed it to her.

"Good," she said. "Bring it over."

I let the doll fall to my side, hanging from my fingers. The niggle in my back stretched around my ribcage and lodged in my solar plexus. She'd want more. I couldn't give it to her.

"I just want to see what you took." I hedged.

"Sure. Sure," she said and grinned.

I felt my brow furrow. Sure, indeed. She could believe what she liked. I flipped the doll over and ripped at the Velcro. There was a tiny screw holding the compartment door shut.

She stretched into a sitting position. "You gotta use your pinky nail."

I stuck my nail in and twisted. The compartment door sprung open.

Her peals of laughter sent a strip of rage up my throat so fast I thought it tore off skin. "What the Hell, Stephanie?"

"There's nothing there. Is there? Is there?"

Indeed. Nothing.

"Never was. Had you going, didn't I?" Her voice was singsong. Joking. She wasn't funny.

"Yeah. You had me going." I wasn't sure if it was relief I felt that she hadn't hid drugs where a kid could find them. I felt something sure as shooting. I just couldn't name it. So. It had to be relief. What else could it have been?

I strode back to where she sat. "Ok," I said patiently. "That was a good one. How about you tell me now?"

She puffed up her cheeks and blew air, an attempt, I supposed, to get serious. "I don't have anything left."

"What was 'anything' then?"

"You know."

"No, I don't."

She jaggled her head up and down. "Yes, you do."

"Ativan?"

She shook her head.

"Dilaudid?"

She grinned. "Getting warmer. Starts with a V and ends with icodin."

"Vicodin," I said.

"And it ends with odka."

"Vodka?"

She nodded.

"You took Vicodin and vodka? Shit we have to call 911." I thought I understood what that earlier sense was that I couldn't name: fear. Instinctual fear. I felt frozen for a second. God. Where the Hell was her phone anyway? I must have done a dozen circles standing in one spot, scanning for it, my arms in the air, my head moving from side to side in a fruitless scan until her laughter came again, hysterical.

"You should see yourself," she said. "You really are worried."

"Hell, yes, Stephanie, I'm worried. Now, where the Hell is the phone?"

"You don't need it."

"I do. I do need it."

She shook her head and waved her hand in front of her face as though she were trying to push air into her lungs. "No, you don't."

"Listen," I said, this time I took the tone of a mother chiding her errant child. "You tell me where that *fuck*-ing phone is. And you tell me right the *fuck* now." I remembered her favored use of the F word, and hoped it would instill some sort of urgency. With luck, it seemed to. She let her hand drop to her lap and she looked at me petulantly.

"I'm just teasing, you, J. I didn't take Vicodin and vodka. You think I'm stupid or something?"

With the relief came the anger. "The thought had crossed my mind."

"You just looked all...I don't know. All high and mighty there when you came in." She rolled over onto her side and pushed herself up to a stand where she weaved to and fro.

Had I been high and mighty? I couldn't remember feeling that way. It was possible I'd forgotten for a moment where I'd come from, what it was like to need a hit to feel normal, why folks turned to junk in the first place. Yeah. I suppose I could have looked that way.

"I just took the Vicodin." She tilted her chin toward the kitchen. "The scrip is on the fridge. Help yourself."

"I-"

"Naw. It's okay. I don't have much but I don't mind sharing." She eyeballed me. "So long as yer not greedy."

I tried to protest but she kept on. "It's not 'cause I want to keep it all, mind. There's other junk too," she said. "I have the vikes for times like this, but I know better than to drink with them." She waved her finger in front of me like a nurse would a naughty boy. "It's bad for you," she said. "To drink and take vikes. Eats up the liver." She tottered over to the kitchen, stumbling once and catching herself on the counter, and reached past the bottle in the front, behind a couple of bags of crumpled and opened potato chips to draw out a smaller baggie like I'd expected to find in the first place: crack, it looked like. The poor man's cocaine. Merciless in its grip on the psyche.

"Times like this?" I asked, registering finally, what she'd said.

She nodded. "Gotta lower my tolerance."

I was starting to get it. "Takes too much junk to get you high now?"

She merely shrugged, but I knew that answer was yes. My guess was during the time she was clean, her body had lost some tolerance for her drug of choice and when she used again, she got high easier. And cheaper. For a short time anyway. I knew from experience that the tolerance rose right back to where it had peaked pretty quickly, no matter how long the abstinent period. The body had its own funny habit of remembering past harms.

She held up the bag. "I'm saving this," she said with a

shrug. "Until my tolerance goes back down but you can have some. Unless you want the vikes. The vikes is good for the pain." She touched her ear as though to indicate my cut.

I felt myself shaking my head.

"You sure?" She took a step toward me, studying me in a way that made me uncomfortable. "You a crackerman or something else?"

I looked at my feet; they seemed to have taken a step or two forward. "Something else," I said. I knew I should have added: not anymore, but I didn't.

She shuffled over to the chair and fell into it, still holding the baggie. I couldn't take my eyes off it and when it swayed in her fingers, I felt a need to grab for it, crumple it in my palm. I took a deep breath instead.

She watched me silently for a while then she said. "I hate myself, you know?"

"Yeah," I said. I did know.

"I hate this shit, too."

I nodded.

"And I love it."

I imagined she did. I knew that as well.

She snuffled then opened her eyes to stare at me. "Pathetic, huh?"

"No," I said. "Just a shame, is all."

"And now I can't even use, it makes me sick."

"Then don't. Don't use." Strange how my mouth felt dry and flooded with saliva all at the same time.

She waggled her head. "No, no. I mean I use, but it's not enough, you know. It's never enough." She sobbed. "Fuck."

I bent down to pick up the offending junk. "It's not good for you."

She shook her head, agreeing with me. "No good at all. Take it away, J. Take it."

I found myself nodding.

"Take it, but leave me the vikes, okay? Leave me the

vikes so I can come off. Can you do that for me? Can you?"

I thought of her comment earlier about her sister's baby being taken away, about her own son being apprehended and the daughter she'd just lost, and I figured she probably had every good excuse to self-medicate, but for her, all that was probably just normal life. Maybe she didn't know life could be any different. She'd find a way to use--harder stuff, maybe--if I took everything from her. I thought of that term, failure to thrive, and I swallowed down my own craving as I looked at the baggie.

"Yeah. I can," I told her.

She sighed and leaned back. "I'll just take a few before bed. Get me through the night."

"No," I said. 'Don't." I had the feeling she was coming down from whatever amount she'd already taken. I'd seen the bottle; there were about thirty in there.

"So how many did you take?"

"Some."

"Some like two?"

She giggled. "Something like that." Then she gave me a wary gaze, guessing perhaps that I was suspicious. "It'll be okay. I'll just take a couple more. Go to bed."

I had the feeling I was being dismissed. "I can't just let you take that shit and go to bed."

"Why not?"

Indeed. She'd probably done a Hell of a lot worse on nights when I didn't know she even existed. "Because I can't."

Her voice went up in tone, singsong. "Sure you can."

"No," I said. "No, I can't. Not now." I gave a mournful thought to my little security blanket that I'd thrown off because of her baby. Gone. Truly gone, that apathy.

She got serious. "You can't stay." She grew harried. "You can't stay here with that junk. You have to get out."

I took a step backwards. "Listen, Stephanie--"

"Listen, nothing. You want to help me, you get that shit away from me. Lock it in your apartment. Don't let me in."

I felt as though someone had poured hot water all down my body. I could have been naked, standing in my shower, the hot faucet sluicing liquid down my back. It would be okay, wouldn't it? I'd been clean long enough. I'd been here, Hell, half an hour or more and I still hadn't opened the bag. Hadn't even thought of crushing down the crystals. Nothing. Shit. Crack wasn't even my drug in the first place. I should be good, really, but if I left it here, she'd just continue on her spiral. At least this way, maybe, just maybe I could help her find sobriety one less Vicodin at a time. Surely that was safer for her.

I closed my eyes briefly, letting the thoughts push out the alarm bells that wanted admittance. It would be okay. I thought of that little girl and wondered if I was doing the right thing for her or not. It had been failing to thrive. Surviving, was all it was doing. It deserved better.

"Ok," I said. "But only if you let me check on you. And only if you let me take the Vikes too."

"Oh, no." She looked frantic at the thought I'd take her pills.

I tried to look firm but kind. I had no idea what that would look like, but tried anyway. "Yeah. You have to."

"Like Hell I do. I don't have to do shit." She flew out of her chair and made to grab the baggie from me.

I avoided her movement and backed up, feeling a stitch in my side where I was still sore and unused to quick movements. I shook the bag at her. "Do you have more?"

She crossed her arms and her bottom lip stuck out stubbornly. I knew if I left her with the pile of pills she'd get desperate and chomp them, maybe half a dozen of them at once. Maybe all of them. Some folks grow their tolerance to junk past what their liver can handle, and I doubted whether she would know the difference if she'd been using crack most of her addiction, if the vikes were just a stop gap to lower her tolerance. I wondered once more how many she'd taken already and how long ago--if she'd need to use again.

"Stephanie. Do you want me to help or were you just

blowing smoke out your ass, 'cause I just don't have time for this." Hell, I didn't even know her well enough to be letting myself care.

She reminded me of a sulky child, aware that she'd been caught doing something bad, but having too much fun to give it up. "Listen," I said. "I'll let you keep the vikes if you agree to do something for me."

She perked up. "Ok."

I waved my hand. "No, no. Don't say okay unless you mean it."

"I do."

"You don't even know what it is yet."

"Doesn't matter. I'll do it."

I chewed the inside of my cheek. Was it really helping, what I planned to do? I knew she could overdose, sure, but more than that, I worried what she would do to her liver if she did plan to use vikes to come off without too much withdrawal pains. What was the good of going clean if you shut down your liver trying to get there?

"You ever extract?"

She looked muddled and I gathered she hadn't. So. She wasn't all that hardcore for all her bluff. "It takes the APAP out of the vike."

I waited for a look of understanding. Not getting one, I went on. "You know, the crap that eats up your liver. You filter it out so that you have a more pure hit but without the extreme mess to your organs. Well," I couldn't help a dark chuckle. "At least somewhat."

I didn't suppose there was any way, really, that you could avoid harming yourself with junk, but at least she wouldn't accidentally shut down her liver trying to get clean. If, indeed, that was what she intended.

I spent the next hour working on a cold-water extract through a scrounged coffee filter she had in the back of her cupboard. I ignored the mess in the kitchen, the unwashed pots that I'd already suspected were there, and the mouse droppings I hadn't. I focused solely on showing her how to safely get the acetaminophen out of her crushed pills in case she decided to jam half a dozen at a time in her mouth, or failing success there, a dozen into her ass.

"You can plug if you want," I said, assuming the worst and that she'd eventually succumb to putting crushed junk into an enema bag when she wasn't getting the high she was used to, and got desperate. "Just portion it out."

By then, a half hour had passed and the junk mix was in the freezer where it could get good and cold.

"But make sure if you do that, to let it come to room temperature first or you'll get more shock than you bargain for. And that's just nasty."

She grinned as she stood there, inspecting the glass that for all intents and purposes looked like ordinary water. I could imagine the bitter taste--another reason to worry she'd plug.

"Are you sure there's junk in there?" She eyed me critically.

"I'm not trying to fool you, Stephanie. There's junk in there. When it's ready, there'll be some little white cloud on the bottom. But don't let it freeze."

"I won't."

I imagined she'd be checking the freezer every five minutes like an impatient kid waiting for homemade Popsicles to solidify, but at least that activity would keep her occupied. At least, I hoped so.

"And don't go downing the lot just because you doubt it's got stuff in it. It does. Okay?"

Another nod and I couldn't help offering a smile. So?" I said. "You're set."

"Yeah. You can go home."

I could go home. I repeated the statement to myself, and felt anxious rather than comforted. Why do you suppose that was? Maybe because I suspected she had other things hiding away. I touched the outside of my pocket and was reassured when I heard the crinkle of plastic from within. She must have watched me and noticed the relief in my face.

"You're gonna take that, right?" she demanded.

"Yup."

"Good. I don't need it. And if I come over banging on your door for it, don't let me in."

"Well, I think I can let you in."

"Oh, no, you can't. You don't know me. You can't let me in."

I imagined the tiny thing, skinny as a crepe laid sideways, trying to wrestle drugs out of me and thought I could laugh. That was, until I remembered how much I felt my soreness with each movement. I saw the almost manic look in her eye that told me she was on the verge of shoving me out the door. Oh, yeah. I saw the want on her. It pimpled the flesh where her skin peeked out from beneath her T-shirt and along her bare arms. And I knew it then. She could easily wrestle the junk away from me.

"No worries," I said. "I'll go out." I wouldn't, but she'd not know that. I'd just strip down to panties and bra and lay on my bed for a spell with the heat turned hard on. Make a nice little sweatshop of my bedroom. Leak the pain from my very pores if I had to. Maybe mix a drink or two. Pretend I didn't have a bag in my pocket. Of course, I shouldn't have to worry about that. It wasn't--was never--my drug of choice. Too low-brow, crack. I enjoyed a finer palette of high. I was a sophisticate.

"I have to get going," I said in a rush and headed for the door. When I had my fingers on the handle I heard her voice behind me and turned.

"Maybe don't go out," she said and waited a spell before finishing. "Just in case."

I knew what the in case meant. "You'll be fine." I stuck my hand in my pocket and squeezed the bag. Just the feel of the slick plastic made me feel better. "You've got enough to get you through the night if you don't get greedy." She had enough to last her a few days, actually.

She nodded. "Greedy. Gotcha." Her breath caught on the last syllable and it looked like she was holding it. Then she stuck up her thumb at me and grinned.

I tried to smile for her, but I had the feeling it came off like a grimace. All I could think of was getting back home and relieving the prickles on the back of my own neck with a good belt of whiskey.

"You'll be fine," I said again, and stepped into the conjoined entryway. A click later and I was into my own apartment, where the familiar smell of massage oils and incense wrapped around me like a soft fleece blanket.

I found I had to swallow down a lot more moisture than usual. Nothing strange, you understand; just the hardcore reaction of a hardcore user in the throes of intended relapse.

Chapter 9

I wanted to make myself a drink and try on some of my favorite underwear. I did, at first. You have to believe me. There was a cute little plaid number with frills on the straps that I'd only worn twice before my gender relapse. I did manage to get a lover to wear it for me one night so I could peel it off her skin in a luxurious delirium of fantasy-style sex, but I'd not got my fingers on it since then.

I ran my palms down a dozen satin bras that hung in my closet or lay draped across mannequins, a half dozen lace ones, and ended up at that simple spandex plaid. I turned it over in my hands and undid the closure. I loved the feel of putting on a good bra, but as a 40 A cup, it never quite did the job unless I could stick in the pads. I tried the matching panties. I shambled into the bathroom to shave beneath my arms because waxing was out of the question with the pain. I even pulled on elbow length gloves--black leather, of course--and shoved on my rhinestone stilettos with the little Playboy bunny on the ankle strap.

I looked, when I checked myself in the full-length mirror, like a beaten up, flat chested man-whore.

I knew the makeup would have made all the difference, but I couldn't go working all that shit onto skin still healing. So I felt like shit. I yanked off the shoes and threw them with a clunk against the wall. I should just fucking give up, is what. I was a pretty boy; I knew that, had accepted it, even, but I still needed to do a lot of work to pass as a woman, and to my overly critical eye, 'pretty boy' wasn't enough at the best of times and now was definitely not a best-of-times moment.

It was inevitable that the crack call to me. You know how that kind of thing is. You force all thought from your mind so that you can run to the activity with a clear conscience. If I don't think about it, you tell yourself, then it's not my fault. I didn't give in; it just sort of, well, happened. As though it was an accident beyond your control. As though a Mac truck had just crept up on you as you quietly and slowly ambled across the street with no more thought of your mortality than an infant would have at being bundled into a Snuggly. As though you didn't have a fucking clue in the first place that jamming your face with junk was exactly what you planned to do all along.

So you tell yourself. So you fool yourself. And so you live with yourself.

I'd like to say the drug was in my hand before I knew it. I'm sure you would like to hear that, but the clear fact is that I knew exactly what I was doing when I plodded down the hallway and crammed my fingers into the pants pocket that I'd left on the bathroom floor before mincing naked to my 'storage closet,' telling myself I was thinking about panties and silk.

I deliberately emptied my mind of any 'gotta take some drugs' thoughts, pulled out the rock and set about sucking it up. Junk: check. Tinfoil: check. Lighter? Not check. I'd thrown that away when I gave up the heroin. Match, yes. That should work. Only it didn't. I couldn't keep it lit long enough. Shit. It seemed I did need a lighter.

I pulled a sweatshirt on over the bra, yanked on a pair of jeans, and crammed my feet into the closest pair of sneakers I could find. A quick trip, that was what. A quick trip to the store to pick up a lighter.

It was foggy and the streetlights had a haze around them that reminded me of a full moon. If I took my time I could make it to the corner store in twenty minutes and maybe the want would be gone by then.

I walked as fast as I could. Time stood still.

I nodded at the wall behind the clerk when I made it there. The lighters were boxed on a shelf to her right. "I need a lighter."

She looked at me, I thought, a little too oddly. "What?" I demanded. My feet shuffled of their own accord.

She shook her head and another patron came up behind me. I felt him near, too near. I moved closer to the counter. "I want a lighter," I said again and she stretched up on her tiptoes to retrieve one from the bin.

"Yellow, orange, or black?"

"Doesn't matter." The gentleman was so close, I could smell the tobacco on him. Stale cigarette smoke and old mint gum. I wanted to tell him to give me some fucken room but I couldn't bring myself to look at anything squarely, let alone turn and face him.

The clerk fished around in the box. "Bic okay?"

"Yes," I scolded. "Any fucken thing. Just get me one."

She gave me a hard look. My gaze dropped to the countertop. I felt myself weaving as though I were drunk. My belly flip-flopped. I skirted my glance back to her; she stood with her hands on her hips. The man crowded me again, and my hands went into my pockets without me thinking about putting them there. I tried to move closer to the counter, out of the way, tried to move sideways out of the way, tried to tried to back up out of the way. I got blocked by his chest.

I knew it in that moment.

They knew, both of them, that I was about to relapse on a drug that I'd always disdained in favor of E or meth or the real bad boy stuff: heroin. Yup. They could see that I'd officially become a loser. As if freak wasn't enough, I had to add crack addict to the label. Yup. I must really want folks to know how screwed up I was. Way to go, J. Knock 'em dead, you skinny bastard, knock 'em dead.

"I just want a lighter," I said and fished for money. There was a crumpled bit of paper in my pocket; I hoped it was a ten or at least a five. How much did those things cost again? I fleeted a look at the patron. "Just a lighter."

"Then get it and get the Hell out of the way," he said. Then he pushed past me so he could dump his handful of items on the counter. I'd been in his way, was all. Nothing more than that. He didn't see the nervousness in my eye, the frantic look that if you'd seen it before, you couldn't mistake. That of desperation. Desperation like I'd seen in Stephanie's eyes. Couldn't have seen it in mine.

It could have been the idea of the desperation that stopped me. I remembered the look in Stephanie's eye, the narrowly focused tunnel-visioned desperation, then I thought of what I'd done to help her come clean bit by bit and I realized that if I did give in, I'd be right back to where she was in a heartbeat. In and wanting out. I didn't think--no, I knew, I didn't have the emotional fortitude, especially now, to beat my way back through that burlap bag.

But it was really the thought of Stephanie's daughter that stuck the skinny side of the wedge in, her and that term. That damned term. Failure to thrive.

I imagined the tiny thing as I'd last seen her, the oddly large head and wasting body. Yes, wasting, I realized now. Too bad for that tiny thing that it couldn't flourish in its own environment. It could take in all the necessities of life and still not thrive. The bird inside my chest chirruped again, and I rubbed it where it ached. I knew I was robbing myself of the ability to take in the right energy.

So. I had to admit that I wanted to use. Shit. I did so want to use.

My tongue stuck to my palette. I had to peel it away and force myself to gather enough spit to swallow. I took a deep breath. I could do this.

"Never mind," I said to the clerk. "Just give me a pack of gum." I put the five-dollar bill on the counter in return for a pack of Juicy Fruit, and then I made my calculated trip back home. I stripped off the offending sweatshirt and jeans because I'd gotten overheated on the walk--overheated and flushed and claustrophobic if you must know--and dropped the clothes in a ball on the hall floor.

My closet was as I'd left it except I'd not noticed I'd dropped the piece of foil I'd shaped into a V. It lay next to one of the mannequins. The toot, another piece of foil, was rolled up into a tube and lay on the floor at my feet. Hell. I'd not even had the decency to settle onto the couch to hit before I discovered the need for the lighter. I'd just squatted on the floor in my 'storage closet' in a way that would have looked obscenely hardcore druggie to any innocent bystander. All around me were pretty things: pink satin sheets draped on quilt racks, white feather boas wrapped around the shoulders of a department store mannequin, I'd salvaged from a shop closure in the city. My lingerie rested in tissue in bags from stores, lay on shelves lined with velvet, and hung from hangers on a circular tie rack I'd jimmied into a bra rack. Panties with lace, panties with gauze, panties with flowery cotton.

Just because I felt ugly didn't mean I had to make this, all this, ugly too.

I found the energy to retrieve and crumple the foil in my hand. The rock inside made a sort of *squinking* sound that put me in mind of tiny evil things dying. Only when I'd got to the door and opened it, stood there in pink panties and plaid bra, and heaved the balled up foil as far as I could to the street, did I feel normal again. It made a ticking sound as it hit the pave of the road. A car whizzed by, crunching it beneath the left front tire. The driver, a burly construction-type worker guy, gave me a weird look: I suppose the sight of an unshaven, bruised up man in bra and panties right out on the front doorstep just didn't register as normal for him.

I turned off every light in my apartment, shuffled all the bras and panties from my storage closet into their respectable cupboards and boxes, closed the door, then shuffled my own shabby self down the few feet of hall to my bedroom. I didn't exactly sleep the sleep of the dead, but at least I felt refreshed enough to brew myself some coffee at eight a.m.

I did feel better. There was more oil in my movements. With the spitting sounds and heated aroma of percolating java filling the apartment, I sent myself for my morning ten-point checkup. A thin brownish line between the stitches on my jaw had appeared: the birth of the scab, finally. My jaw line had shifted back like tectonic plates into a shape recognizable as the old J. My hair would cover most of it as I grew it out, assuming I'd want to have long hair in my femme state. I wasn't sure; there was something about that ultra-feminine look that I resisted.

Clothes could be changed at a whim, I knew: I feel froufrou today, they could say, or I just feel damned sloppy, but regardless of the mindset, still the person underneath would be a woman. It's just that clothes helped people react and act to me in a way that made me comfortable.

I hated the word tranny. It meant I was in the midst of something--on my way to something else. On my way to normal, as if I wasn't normal in the first place. As if something was wrong with me. Those words and labels the queer community pasted onto its members were as inhibiting as the prejudices the rest of society taped onto our asses. I spared a thought for Molly who, despite her stubborn insistence that she was a proud gay woman, was still not comfortable in her own skin--so much so that it had become her own personal mission to convert every straight woman she met to prove how 'normal' she really was. It was a trap we'd somehow got ourselves into, that we wanted to show how normal our lives were to the people whose values we eschewed.

It was the other stuff that wasn't normal: the addictions, the self-mutilations. Those were just behaviors. I could change those.

I heard the final death throes of the coffee machine signaling the last bit of water had been spasmed from its depths. I took a quick pee sitting down, and after completing all the requisite pieces of the toilette, moved with significant ease to the kitchen. If heaven had a smell, I think it would have to be coffee.

It was only when I was pouring that I realized I'd actually left Stephanie alone all night. The start of realization bade me put the pot back on the element. I hadn't heard from her. I hadn't heard her.

I stared at a spot on the backsplash for what seemed a half dozen minutes. I had to go over.

I didn't want to.

I picked up my mug and set it down again. She'd expect me to check on her. I wanted to check on her. I picked my mug up, thinking even as I did, that I was wrong. I did not want to check on her. If I went over there and I found her juiced out of her mind, I could probably handle that; I'd seen enough of that kind of thing, been in that state enough, that it would actually be comforting to see. Nothing I couldn't handle, you understand. But if she'd given in and called in some reinforcements for the vikes, and if I went over and found her staring off into space with as much sense of interest as a glazed donut, tired from tweaking all night, then I wasn't sure I'd have the emotional fortitude to be sweet and comforting.

An addict in recovery is one thing; an addict relapsing is quite another. And if you really must know, neither was one I wanted to deal with.

I avoided going over all morning. I drank five cups of coffee, paced back and forth from living room to kitchen to bedroom where I could listen at the wall, and was shoveling four more scoops into a new filter when the door received three sharp raps. I froze where I stood, hand deep in the bag of Nabob grounds, trying to scrape out the last of what was in there.

It was Stephanie; I knew it. She'd made it through the night and had come to show me her own sense of fortitude.

Sure. That was it. Or it could be Stephanie come to beg me for the crack she'd left with me. I immediately regretted rifling through the cupboard to make and drink my coffee; I must have made too much noise and she knew I was home. Why had I got involved again?

The sounds came again followed by a female voice, muffled by the inch or so of wood.

"Jay. Jay, are you home? Dammit you fucken jerk, answer the fucken door."

My reluctance fell to dread: not Stephanie--Molly. Much, much worse at the moment.

"Hold your horses," I bellowed as I made my way down the hall. A responding thump met me as I drew close. I yanked the door open, hand on my hip beneath my floral housecoat, purposely showing her the cream-colored nightie I had on.

She pursed her lips. "So. You're all womanly now, huh?"

She pushed in without really looking at me and flipped the edge of my robe in her typical teasing way. Then she grabbed at it and held onto the edge, holding it open. I knew the bruises on my side and on my collarbone had turned yellow, and while somewhat faded, were still plainly visible.

I pretended they weren't there even as she stood there gawping at them. Then she brought her gaze to my face for the first time and made a small sound that struck me as a gulp.

"So?" I demanded. "You thinking you'd want to hump me now I'm a woman?" I yanked my robe from her fingers and held myself haughty and high. "Well, I ain't got time for that this morning. And even if I did, I wouldn't feel like it."

Take that, I thought and closed the door with a bit more force than it needed. I walked back up the hall without asking her in or acknowledging her further. Coffee waited. If she wanted to be nice, she could have some.

She spoke from behind me, obviously ignoring my boorishness in favor of haranguing me in that way she had that would sound like rudeness to someone else, but that I recognized as concern. Damn her; I didn't want to do this. Not this. Not with her.

"What happened? Who did that to you? When did it happen; last weekend? Looks old."

I threw a noncommittal comment over my shoulder.

Her voice: closer. "That tells me nothing, Jay."

"It tells you exactly what I want to tell you." I lifted my mug off the sideboard where I'd left it in my quest for more coffee. I drained the last three mouthfuls of icy java as though it tasted like ambrosia, then made all the purposeful preparations for another pot.

"You can't ignore me."

I wouldn't look at her. "Who says?"

I filled the pot with water from the tap and poured it into the back of the percolator then snapped the on button. I wouldn't turn around to face her. I couldn't anyway; I was trembling.

I felt her hand on my shoulder, warm and moist. Gentle.

"Stupid lizzy," I managed to get out before the rattle of grief overtook the clarity, and her arms went round my waist before I could catch my breath. It was so unexpected, and so intimate that I couldn't stop the sob that escaped my throat. Damn it all if she didn't squeeze in reply, pressing her entire front into my back.

"So you do want to hump me," I said trying to joke, and hating the sound of tears in my voice.

"You stupid tranny," she said.

I felt her nose against my neck, her words a hot bit of air on my skin.

"Your mouth got you in trouble again, huh?"

All I could do was nod like some pitiful loser.

"Bastards," she said.

I waggled my head up and down.

"I'd feel bad for you if I thought you didn't deserve it." She pinched me playfully on the waist. I slapped her hand away.

"Did you mouth off to some big boys, Jay?'

"Yes."

"And did you insult their manhood?"

"Yes." I smiled this time, reluctantly.

"And were they so worried for their sexuality that they felt the need to kick the certainty out of yours?

"Yes, they did." Petulant now, coming round, thankful she hadn't made a show of my tears.

She made a sound like a grunt, as though she agreed, but nevertheless, was surprised at the truth of what we both knew. "They never have been able to take that."

She let go my waist and moved away to let me gather my dignity. She crossed her arms, more I thought as an effort to steel herself, than to seem defensive.

She nodded to indicate my nightgown. "You got some goo on ya."

I looked down; there was a spot of something that looked like grease on the breast cup. I shrugged. "Guess I drool in my sleep."

She smiled but there was no humor in it. For the first time, I noticed she hadn't spiked her hair this morning; it lay in dregs against her skull, short but clumpy as though styling products had glued it there and she couldn't wash it out. Her cheeks looked sunken in and the smudges of gray under her eyes told me she hadn't slept for a while. Hadn't eaten.

She saw my scrutiny and seemed to deflect it. "So," she said. "I imagine you didn't beg them to stop."

I shook my head at her statement. "No begging for this pretty boy. Or girl," I corrected.

A smile, forced, it seemed this time, spread across her face and she licked her finger to strike a mark in the air. "Score one for the tranny, then."

"Not much of a score," I said. As much as I hated the word, it didn't sound so bad coming out an old lizzie's mouth.

She sighed, exhausting the possibility that things could have gone anywhere different with the gay bashers; after all, we'd had the discussion dozens of times before.

"Well, that's what I like about you, Jay," she said. "You don't take shit no matter if you win or lose." She paused as the coffee machine spurted. "There enough in there for me?"

I supposed she'd been nice enough. I reached for the cupboard. "Yeah."

"The one with the boobs," she said as my hand went into the recesses of the third cupboard where I kept the mugs. I peeked out from beneath my upraised arm to see her make for the fridge to get the cream I knew she'd load into it. She looked fatigued as she moved, not her usual frenetic self.

"Don't give me the one with that stupid cartoon on it," she complained. "You know I hate that shit."

I pushed aside a couple of mugs and reached for the back of the shelf where I kept the novelty mugs I saved for certain company. I bypassed the 'Straight but not narrow' and grabbed the one with the huge titties on the side, the one Molly said she liked because she enjoyed the feel of boobies against her chin.

I poured half a cup of the java and passed the mug to her so she could fill the rest with cream. I grimaced at the thought of it, knowing it would taste milky and weak.

"So why are you here?" The question that I wanted to ask was, what's wrong, but I knew she'd be about as forthcoming with that news as I was with details of my beating.

She adjusted the mug so all of her fingers went through the handle and her thumb curved around the cup. "I missed you."

"You really pissed me off."

She sighed. "And here I was worried you were hurt."

"I was hurt." I stomped on the words as they came out, hating the rise in pitch that made me sound defensive.

"Well, I can see you were hurt, asshole."

"No, Molly. Hurt as in emotionally." Strange. It was easier to admit to that than to the physical discomfort.

"As in I hurt you." She stressed the I.

"Yeah."

"Not as in hurt by the big bad boys that beat the living freaken crap out of you."

She returned my accusing stare but slipped her typical grin over top of it, then let it go when she saw I wasn't having any of it.

"Well, that too." I rubbed my side and opened the flap of my robe. I eased closer, brushing the largest, sorest bruise, the one that stretched up from behind the spaghetti straps, with my palm. "This will heal," I said.

"And the pain I caused won't, I suppose."

I shrugged.

"Look Jay. I imagine you are pissed, but you know I don't hold anything back."

"I suppose we all have our weaknesses."

"Strengths. They're my strengths, Jay. Just like your big mouth, which also, I might add, doesn't hold anything back-- gets you into so much fucking trouble. Sheesh. You really should know better."

"What, and let them get away with it?"

"Why not. What does it matter?"

"Well, for starters, they were gonna beat the freak out of me anyway."

She scoffed. "If only it was that easy, huh?"

I said nothing.

She pressed on. "So you closed up your only possible escape route."

"Hell no. There was no escape, you stupid dyke." Maybe I shouldn't have pulled out the D word, but there it was all the same, stinking in the open air.

She waggled her finger at me, feigning a nanny scolding an errant child, knowing that the child has been naughty, but too indulgent to do anything about it.

Without showing any amount of pique, she tilted the mug to her mouth and took a big swallow. The boobs of the mug pressed into her chin as she upended, leaving little nipple dents. The sight of it made me choke down a chuckle. Damn her.

"You see," she started. "What you fail to comprehend--"

"So look who's using polysyllables now."

She quirked a thick black brow at me, nonplussed at my interruption. "What you fail to comprehend," she continued, "is that there is always an escape. You just choose to confront."

"Like you don't."

"I can afford to confront." She flexed her bicep for me, then stretched both her arms out sideways in a full flex, the boob mug slopping coffee out the top and onto the floor as she did so. "See these rifles."

"I think you mean guns."

"Guns? That's stupid. Mine are rifles. Quick. Accurate."

I shook my head. "How can you be so butch and not know the right lingo, Molly. So, yeah, what about those rifles."

She shrugged. "Would you mess with them?"

I moved to inspect one. "Yeah. Maybe. This one looks like it could use some work."

She brought the mug down and when I thought she would clunk it against my skull, she placed it delicately on the sideboard. Neither of us said anything for a moment. She seemed to be watching me, waiting for something, and it felt awkward. I wanted to say something but couldn't come up with the words. I thought about telling her about the baby next door, that I wanted to help Stephanie so I could see the little thing make a decent go at thriving. Something kept me from it, though.

With the same hand as had held the mug, she pushed her fingers into my robe. They burrowed beneath the strap and moved down. I felt the surprising softness of her touch on my bottom rib. "You can't take too many more of these, Jay."

I almost bolted backwards, so surprised was I at this second touch. Instead, I willed myself to stay put and nodded. "I know."

Her fingers found an old scar between my last rib and the second to last, one of many that lay a railroad track of ties up my side to beneath my armpit. It felt odd, her touch there. Almost real, but distant, not quite numb. You know, the way old scars feel and yet don't feel. Her fingers walked up my ribcage like a pianist touching keys in a familiar melody.

"You do more damage to yourself than they do," she said. "It's like you want them to try to hurt you more than you can hurt yourself."

I pulled away from her and wrapped my robe tight, crossing the right panel straight over the left and belted it there with my arms.

"Is that what you get for a whole semester of dating a first year Psych student? Who needs to pay tuition when you can hump an undergrad?"

"I wasn't humping her. I was rocking her world."

"Right. Till she went back to her boyfriend."

"Don't change the subject."

"Okay then," I said. "Since we're on the subject of not changing subjects, why are you here, Molly?"

"I told you."

"You told me you missed me."

"I did."

"Maybe you did, but you look like you haven't slept in days." The shot hit home; I could tell by the way she made a grab for her mug again and shoved it toward her mouth without any sense of finesse. She couldn't meet my gaze.

"So?" I pressed. "What is it?"

"You really are a jerk."

"Bitch," I corrected. "Bitch sounds better."

"Right. Because you're a woman now." A tease, but with the familiar edge of contempt in her voice that was purposeful. A way to deflect attention.

"You're changing the subject again."

Her tone went up a notch. "No, I'm not. You changed it."

The accusation wasn't lost on me. She wanted to drop the burden of conversation back onto me. My hurts. My Hell. God forbid she let anyone peek into hers.

I refused to let her make me feel defensive. "You're still changing the subject."

She glared at me. Her thin top lip all but disappeared.

"Come on, Molly. What's wrong? Why are you here?" Nothing like an attack when one feels cornered. You know, to get the blood going.

She wouldn't answer; instead she sipped at her mug as though the last dregs of coffee were still as warm and as fragrant to the tongue as the aroma was to the air. I knew better. Mine had long gone cold. She couldn't fool me. And she couldn't rile me up either, with her nonchalance, her pretension of normalcy. I'd just turn it right back on her. You know how folks hate it when you act like you don't care. Drives them crazy.

"Okay. You're gonna make me guess, and I've had a Hell of a few days, so you know I'm gonna guess crazy. Like: Police, jail. Oh, I know. You got some girl pregnant..."

She had the decency to grin, but it didn't last but a few split seconds before it faltered and the thin top lip was trembling in time with the chin that still sported the nipple dents. It was seconds before I realized what was happening.

"You never cry," I said, stupidly, and as I said it, I knew that she was indeed crying. Her whole face crumpled and I felt compelled to go to her, and frozen by shock at the same time.

"Molly?" I said, and the sound of uncertainty in my own voice made the ringing of the doorbell sound musical and intimate. It took me a second to realize I had someone at the door and that the normal thing would be to answer it.

I took a step toward Molly, reached out. I felt her back away so she could press into the counter.

Banging started, coming from the door. Insistent. The bell ringing.

Of course, you know it was Stephanie. Of course, you

know she was jonesing.

Of course, you know I didn't have her stuff.

Chapter 10

"I did what you told me," Stephanie said without so much as a hello or a 'how was your night', as though she had no idea about the struggle her junk posed me. To be fair, she couldn't know, but that didn't make her rude interruption any more welcome.

"Good," I said, holding open the door and sending furtive glances over my shoulder to see if Molly was okay.

Stephanie looked me up and down, obviously taking in the satin nightgown that stretched across my flat chest, and lost what she was going to say.

"So?" I demanded, noting the way her stare had stopped at the bulge in the middle of my nightie.

There was a quirk of her brow before she recovered her manners--and control of her gaze--and was able to speak.

"So, it worked."

She fidgeted where she stood. I noticed she was barefoot. The toenails were black and dirty. I had to hold back an outward shudder of revulsion. I looked down at my own toes: not painted and pink, but trimmed at the very least. Nice straight lines to avoid the dreaded ingrown nail syndrome. The hair on my big toe had lightened from the repeated waxings over the years. She followed my gaze, keeping up a frenetic stream of words as though she were trying to recover from a horrible faux pas. Or maybe from a night of tweaking out on distilled drugs.

"I did it like twice through the night and it helped some and then I got to thinking it would be better to just you know....try it another way...it's awful bitter, you know. Hard to drink. So I--"

"So you plugged, is what you're trying to say," I said, impatient and unable to find enough empathy for her, knowing Molly was still in the kitchen, probably wiping at her eyes, and that the moment she was about to come clean would never return. Some sixth sense I'd always wished for had begun to bud, and it was a hard jabbing sense in the back of the neck.

"What does that have to do with me?"

She stared at me. "Well because you have the rest of my stuff."

"You told me not to give it to you."

"I don't want to use, J."

I looked at the hard way she stood, the gaunt look to her face. She was lying. "Then what?"

"I--" She gave me a wincing look that was more of a confession than her words could be.

"You what?" I pressed.

"I ran out."

I examined her with narrowed eyes: dirty feet, uncombed hair, same pajama pants as the day before. I could tell by her pupils she was not all the way down; on her way, maybe, but not all the way there.

"You look okay," I said warily because those things that for many would add up to a bad night, would actually point in favor of an addict's recovery, and yet...something in her eyes bade me use caution. "Make it through alright?"

She nodded almost too quickly. "Yeah. Yeah, I did."

"You sleep at all?" I couldn't believe I was engaging her. Damn fool, I was.

She nodded again, this time her words were as staccato as her head bobbing. "Yeah, yeah. Fell asleep after the last batch. Right about 3 a.m."

I did some quick calculations, painfully aware that she was still standing in the porch and the door was still far too open. Part of me wanted to invite her in, but a bigger, much more cautious part kept me from doing so. I prodded her again.

"If you had the last batch at three, you must be feeling back to normal about now."

Her gaze swerved away and she picked at her nails. Some brownish gunk stood out on the back of the nail that had dredged in. "Maybe some. But I'm good, J. I'm good."

"Then what do you want?"

"You're pretty rude for a guy that has a bag full of junk at his disposal. Or did you smoke it up? Did you, did you smoke my stuff you fucken--?"

"I'm not a guy," I said.

That stopped her tirade cold. "Huh?"

"I'm not a guy," I repeated. "I'm a gal." I ran my hand down my side much like I'd done for Molly except I did not open the flap of my robe all the way this time. It was enough that the front was open and that she could see the beautiful creamy nightie I had on. I struck a model's pose for her, wanting a reaction, daring one.

The confusion for the moment seemed to steal all her aggression and it softened her features. She looked okay, right then. I thought things would be alright.

"Holy fuck," she said.

"Indeed."

"What are you, some sort of he/she?"

I heard a crunching sound from behind me: Molly came up on my back, smacking on a cracker she'd obviously rummaged from the cupboard. "What's up?"

Her face was still puffy from the tears, but she'd made a quick recovery, it seemed, in light of company and decided to make an appearance.

"Stephanie wants to know if I have a dick and a vagina."

Molly queered up her face. "Nope," she said between munches. "She's got nothing." She grinned a fake grin at me.

Stephanie looked even more confused. "So you're a--"

"Don't even think it," I interrupted before she could say the dreaded E word. "I most definitely have genitalia; it just doesn't match what I am."

"Oh." She seemed to accept that. "Explains a lot."

Molly stopped chewing. "Really?" she said. "'Cause it doesn't make a lick of sense to me."

She jabbed me in the arm and went her way back up the hall to the living room muttering to herself that she'd never figure me out in a million years. I could hear her jangling through the utensil drawer. I mentally added the knowledge that I had some coolers in the fridge, to the Molly I knew would decide quite quickly to evaporate tears with alcohol, and ended up with a solution that ended in a Hell of an afternoon.

At least the notion of my gender had sidetracked Stephanie enough to ward off the jonesing anger that had beset her. It felt safe to let her in, to see if our little experiment had helped. I thought of the strange little infant, it's perfect ears, the reason I'd decided to set about this path in the first place. I mean, someone had to think about her, look out for her.

"You might as well come in," I told Stephanie.

"Yeah, sure," she said but didn't move.

"I have to close the door sometime," I said.

She glanced at the handle and the way my hand was clenched around it. She looked back up into my face. "You got my stuff?"

I nodded toward the heavier outside door just beyond our mutual entryway. "It's out there."

"Out there?"

I shrugged. "In the street."

It looked like she'd bolt for the road but something held her back. She narrowed her gaze at me. "You sell it?"

I shook my head. "Threw it out."

"Oh great." She shuffled inside and leaned against the wall, defeated. "You threw it out."

"Threw it out."

"You remember where? Can I find it?"

I laughed. "Sure you can. It hasn't moved since it got squashed."

"What do you mean?"

"I mean a few dozen cars have run over it by now." As I said it, I realized squashed would mean crumbled, crumbled would mean powdered. Powdered would mean totally unruined as far as she was concerned: smokeable, snortable, pluggable, or any other old thing she wanted to do with it. I had to grab at that bit of smoke I'd accidentally let go and try to jam it back in its bottle before she actually did run out into the street and rummage for the foil.

"Actually," I said hastily. "It's gone. I saw some guy pick it up a few minutes after I chucked it out there."

"You said--"

"I know what I said. I was joking."

"It's not funny."

"I know."

She let out a heaving sigh and slipped down the wall, where she lifted her knees so her chin could rest on them. "I'm glad it's gone."

I eased myself down next to her. I still hurt in various places, but movement had grown steadily easier over the last twelve hours: a sure sign I was on the mend, at least physically.

"It goes away, you know."

She looked at me, her eyes red, desperate. "Does it?"

"Sure it does. You remember don't you?"

She closed her eyes, thoughtful and let go a lengthy breath. "Not really."

I gave that comment some thought. "Well, it goes away in spurts," I said.

"How long?"

"How long are the spurts?"

"No, how long have you been clean?"

I could have answered to the minute if I wanted. "Not long enough," is what I said.

Chapter 11

We sat in the living room putting plastic cheese slices onto melba toast and drinking coolers. Mine, a pomegranate one with vodka, was nearly gone and the straw I was drinking it through was chewed flat so that the rest slurped its way into my mouth. We'd been sitting there, all three of us, for at least an hour, saying precious little in between crunching and slurping.

It had been Molly's idea, actually. When Stephanie and I had not moved from our spot on the floor's hallway, she'd shuffled down in a pair of pink, fuzzy slippers that I knew I'd left next to the couch a few days ago. She held a cooler in one hand: pineapple, I think, complaining that all I had in my fridge were girlie drinks. She took one look at us sitting there and said, "You two are freaking me out."

She ushered us onto the couch and demanded to know why I bought crappy cheese slices instead of real cheddar. "And this shit," she'd said, shaking the Melba toast box at me, "is the devil's handmaiden. They're fucken bland, Jay. Whatever would possess you to buy such rotten snacks?"

Stephanie had giggled and Molly, realizing she had found a new audience, had put on her best come-hither smile and set about the wooing thing she did with new acquaintances. She wanted everyone to like her. At least until she'd decided whether or not she liked them: then she didn't care. But for now, Stephanie was an unknown and Molly spent all of ten minutes gathering stuff onto plates and hugging three coolers into the living room.

She passed one to each of us. While I secretly worried Molly would be sizing Stephanie up for conquest, Stephanie was following Molly everywhere with her eyes. I doubted she was queer, but I also knew that Molly had something about her that drew people, and she'd won over more than her share of heterosexual women. It was a specialty, in fact; like Rachael Ray was good at cooking meals out of nothing, Molly was good at creating curiosity where there was no curiosity before. No wonder she thought every woman was secretly queer.

Regardless of Stephanie's orientation, that was the last thing either of them needed. I wasn't sure what I should be doing: ask my next door neighbor to leave and suffer the worry she'd be out in a second looking for crack, or ask her to stay and have a drink with a lesbian bent on bending her over.

I decided the best I could do under the circumstances was to sit like a wedge, emotionally, between them.

"I'm not sure I should be drinking this early," I said, really meaning that I didn't think we should be drinking in front of Stephanie.

"Then don't," Molly said. Flopping down onto the chair in the corner and lifting a bottle to her mouth. "But I am dying for this." She pulled a long draft off the mouth, eyeing Stephanie all the while. If she so much as licked her lips after that drink, I was going to get up and pummel her.

Stephanie seemed not to share my worry that alcohol might be a trigger for her. Maybe she thought the booze would soften the edge of detox, I didn't know. I just knew she downed her cooler in record time and reached for the one I'd put on the table, unsure as I was as to just what I should be doing. I made a grab for it as her hand curved around the bottle.

"You sure that's a good idea?"

Molly's voice came. "Narc, Jay. Sheesh."

I turned to her. "Well, is it a good idea, Molly?"

She shrugged. "Hell if I know; what do you think, Steph?"

Stephanie pursed her lips and said, "Good idea or not; if I don't get something in me, I'm going to heave."

"Oh," I said and passed her the bottle. In my befuddled state, I'd forgotten what it was like to be detoxing: the shits, if there was any description for it at all. Better to give her some booze than to have her succumb to the pains and make a run for drugs.

"I've got another in the fridge, I think."

The dreaded pomegranate one, if I remembered correctly, which is what I ended up drinking through a straw because I hated the flavor, and the straw would get the booze past my palette without having to taste too much. We sat there, like I said, for almost an hour, and I was watching the two of them as though one would swoop down on the other like Dracula on his newest victim. I felt very much as though all the unfinished, unspoken business was swarming around like a buzz of locusts ready to devour my sanity. Neither of them seemed aware of any haze of bugs real or imagined, which I supposed was a good thing given Stephanie was probably about three hours off any meds.

My uneasiness grew with each quiet moment. Molly undoubtedly had shelved whatever had brought her here, but it was roaming her mind in laps, I could tell. Stephanie kept equally quiet, but when she started twitching about an hour and five minutes in, I knew she'd not been entirely honest with me, and that she'd kept some drugs hidden in her apartment. I should have known. An addict is an addict is an addict. And addicts can't be trusted. Not ever.

I was reclining on the sofa, across from Stephanie who sat on the opposite end, and diagonally to Molly, who sat cross-legged in the armchair in the corner. The Melba toast box, empty, lay discarded on the floor where she'd thrown it, and there was a litter of plastic cheese wrappers on the floor all around. Stephanie began to scratch at her elbows, running her nails down her forearm and back up, raking slowly, deliberately. This was a good indicator for me, but when she started rubbing her stomach, I knew the jig was up.

"You need to use," I said.

She didn't deny it. She bit her bottom lip, ashamed, it seemed, and nodded.

"You ever do anything to such excess that you feel really sick after?"

"Hasn't everyone?" I said.

"Amen," Molly said from over in her corner.

"No," Stephanie said. "Not like that. Like eating too much, like making yourself sick on purpose so you could eat some more."

"Like the Romans. Stuck feathers down their throats, didn't they?" Molly said.

Stephanie looked annoyed. "Then it's like buying a Texas Mickey and drinking so much you have to get your belly pumped."

"Ha," said Molly raising her bottle in salute. "Been there."

Stephanie sighed. "Okay then. It's not like that. Not like any of that." She grabbed her lip with her teeth again, adjusted her position so she could hold onto her stomach better.

"It's like you've fantasized about sex to the point where you've imagined things you could never, ever do and it still isn't enough. You want more. You fantasize more. You take yourself to an edge where you'd be sick if you physically did those things?"

"Honey," Molly interrupted. "I wrote the book."

"You're not getting it." Stephanie complained.

"Sweetie," I said to her. "I think what you're missing is that we do get it. We get all of it."

She seemed to think about that. "Shameful excess," is what she said, and I thought it was the perfect description.

"Yeah," I said. "Exactly."

She nodded. "I blew coke all night. Every few minutes-- maybe 30--in between. Soon's I felt myself come down, I blew more. God."

"It's okay," I said.

"No, it's not."

"No?"

"No, because I'm hitting hard, guys. I'm really hitting hard."

"Sick?" I asked.

"Getting pretty." Her eyes welled up. Tears dribbled down one side of her face while the other pooled before running straight down. "Oh, God. It's bad."

"It's okay," I said, getting up. I caught Molly's eye and it looked panicked. "What?" I asked her. "What?"

"We have to get her something."

"Like Hell we do."

"Jay, we have to. If she's been doing all she says, she's gonna hit real hard. We can't help her here."

"Then she needs detox. Safe detox."

"No, No." Stephanie popped up from the couch. "You can't send me there. You can't. You can't."

"You have to go," I said.

"Just give her something, Jay. Send her on her way."

"Send her on her way? Are you fucking crazy, Molly?"

Molly got up from her chair and took me by the still robed arm. She pulled it hard, dragging me in the direction of the kitchen. "You have to get rid of her," she said, close to my ear.

I yanked my arm from her clutch. "Get rid of her?"

She nodded. "And fast."

"The Hell I will. She needs help. We have to help her. Remember, Molly?" I didn't want to bring my own past to her mind, but there it was. I had somehow enmeshed my own misery with this young girl. With this young girl and a baby I didn't know.

"Honey, I'd do anything for you, but this chick needs help we can't give." Molly leaned away from me, craning her neck so she could at least make a peek toward the living room to check on Stephanie.

"It's okay. She's lying on the couch," she said, as though I'd asked. Then she moved close again. "Listen, Jay. We can't help her. And pretty soon she's going to know that."

"So?"

"So, she's gonna get pretty insistent."

"Yah, well I happen to know a pretty strong woman can take her."

Molly didn't even break a smile and I wondered for a second where her constant humor had gone. "It's not that," she said. "She's going to really want. She's going to need. Do you really want to have someone coming down that badly here? Can you take it? What if she gets sick?"

"She will. You know she will."

"I know. But I mean really sick. What if she still has some on her?"

I blew my lips with disbelief. If Stephanie had any rock left, she'd be smoking it, not moaning on my couch. I didn't want to admit that I'd taken Stephanie's word that there was no more in her apartment, didn't want to show Molly that I'd failed that little test.

Molly grabbed my arm again. "Listen, Jay. You've been off the scene for a while. I know that. And you know I've not cleaned myself up yet--"

"Yet?"

She waved off my hopeful echo. "But what you don't know is how potent some of that stuff can be. She hid all that powder or whatever the Hell she's been blowing all night--she hid that from you, and gave you the shitty old crack to throw you off, who's to say she doesn't have a pick-me-up in her pocket. You know. Just in case.

"I think she came to get the crack because she wanted to hold off on using up the last of her stash. I think she hoped you had something else. Now she knows--"At this point, Molly leaned back toward the doorjamb again before she'd continue and when she leaned back, her voice grew hoarse and secretive.

"Now she knows you don't have anything. She might blow the last bit."

"So the longer we keep her, the better off she'll be. Clean her system up."

"Oh, poor naïve, Jay. Have you really forgotten what it's all like?"

I thought for a minute, walked myself back to some pretty shameful and desperate times. With the pause to think instead of react, I knew what to do. "Yeah," I said. "You're right."

"Duh."

"I'll call Sherona."

"Yeah, call--what the Hell? What do you mean 'call Sher-onimo? Who the Hell is Sher-onimo and why the Hell would we phone him? We need to get little Miss Thing outta here."

"Sherona. She's the girl who--" I stopped mid-sentence. Molly didn't know the half of what went on that night we'd been at the bar. She hadn't met Sherona except to point her out to me. "She's the black girl from the bar."

I expected Molly to give me a knowing look, maybe half a dozen innuendoed comments.

To her credit, she didn't. Instead she said. "Call her."

"Good. You watch 'Little Miss Thing.' I'm going to look for Sherona's number."

Molly gave me a look that said she didn't believe anything would help, least of all call some score from the bar, but she would humor me.

"She's a nurse," I said.

"Of course." Molly shrugged. "A nurse is just absolutely and indubitably the person to call. You go." She used her fingers to shoo me away. "You go now. Go do the right thing."

"It'll be okay," I tried to assure her but she'd already started back into the living room, showing me her back. I took a breath. Maybe she was right. Maybe this was too much for me. For her. For anyone but the detox unit, but I knew it was the best I could do. I remembered hitting my bottom. It had looked nothing like this. It was messy and painful and almost unsurvivable. If I could spare that for Stephanie, I could breathe again. Somehow I just knew I could breathe again. I had to try to help.

My room was a shamble of clothes pulled out and tossed aside. A quick survey told me I'd have to dig for the jeans I had on the night of the beating. The beating. Had I come only a few days away from there? It felt already like an eternity. But it wasn't. It was days. Mere days. Surely Sherona would remember me.

I kicked aside a pile of socks I'd washed and placed on the chair the night I went out, thinking I'd put them away the next morning. I hadn't, of course, because of 'the incident' as I was now thinking of it. The pile had since leaned sideways like the Tower of Pisa and toppled over onto the laminated floor. The Converse sneakers had ended up somehow separated one from the other: one in the corner and one peeking out from beneath the bed, its white toe a ghost of rubber and dirt. There was a splash of blood on the toe that I'd not noticed before and I absently kicked it further under the bed. I used my foot to sort through the socks and the one neat bit of white boxer briefs that must have been in the pile.

There they were, the jeans--beneath the socks and underwear, in a crumpled mess I'd not given a thought to since I'd peeled them off. I jammed my hand into one pocket then the next, finding within two pieces of rumpled up paper: the doctor's information and the number. I already felt a weight slip down my back and thud to the floor. I scrambled to the phone. Dialed. It rang. I wasn't aware I was clenching the receiver until I heard her voice and my fingers immediately went slack.

"Sherona?"

"Yes." Her tone was hesitant, I realized. She didn't recognize my voice. Of course she didn't; she'd only spent a few minutes--maybe 15--with me. While she'd talked a good deal that night, I'd remained fairly quiet, uttering one-worders. I found myself stumbling into the silence.

"It's J. You know? From the other night?"

"Oh good God. Are you okay?"

There went the second weight thudding to the floor: she remembered me. Yes. Yes, I could be okay.

"Better," is what I said.

"Oh, I'm glad."

"I'm glad I caught you. You weren't out the door, were you?"

"Just got off a clinical shift. Ten hours. Not so bad." I thought I could hear the shrug in her voice.

I wasn't sure how I could ease the conversation toward what I needed from her. Best to just let fly. "Listen, Sherona, I'm sorry to phone you like this--"

"Don't be. I was thinking about you all week."

"Really?" I felt a twinge of interest at that, despite the desperate situation.

"Really," she said. "You heal up okay? It looked like a pretty bad beating."

"Pretty much. It always heals," I said dismissively. "But I wanted to ask you something."

"Ask away."

"I need a favor."

"Shoot."

I hesitated, but at her insistence ended up blurting the whole damn thing as well as the question that had brought me to her. I expected her to hang up or curse like she'd done in the bar's bathroom; I felt my whole body tense with the expectancy of it.

"Where do you live?" is what she said and the third weight dropped onto my toe. I could laugh if it wouldn't sound so maniacally relieved.

I gave her my address and placed the receiver back onto the end table. So much for that. She'd be here in about 10 minutes she'd said. Ten minutes. It would fly by, surely. I glanced at the clock: 12:30. Lunchtime. Maybe I should make everyone a snack. I started back up the hall, fully intending to check on Stephanie and Molly, hoping one would be quietly sitting in a chair and the other doing Florence Nightingale stuff like wiping a cloth across a sweaty brow and murmuring calming, soothing words.

You can imagine what I did see.

Both were on the floor. Stephanie had a hold of Molly by the throat, and Molly's wonderful self-proclaimed, rifle-quick biceps were pinned beneath the weight of Stephanie's knobby knees.

I didn't think. I just cursed. "Jesus Jesus Jesus." Stephanie, hearing me, shot a look my way. Her knees pressed deeper as she planted her second hand over Molly's mouth.

"She tried to hit me."

"This has got to be a nightmare," I said and stomped over, annoyed more than anything else, to wrestle Stephanie off my burly protector. Before I could get within a foot of her, she yelped in pain and whipped her hand from Molly's mouth.

"You fucken dyke," she said, glaring down at Molly.

Molly ignored the comment in favor of speaking to me, her constant calm giving her a weird aura of Buddha-esque serenity. "She's pretty wiry."

"Yeah, right." I made a grab for Stephanie's arm and got scratched on the back of my hand for my trouble. I wished I'd thought to get dressed before coming back into the room; the silk nightie was not exactly tousling attire.

"I come here for help and you do this to me?" Stephanie, wiry as she was, had a good sense of balance. I couldn't shift her off Molly's legs.

"We are helping you."

"By trying to pin me to the couch. Fuck. What kind of help is that?"

"No one is trying to pin you--" I glared down at Molly

as I registered the words. "You try to hold her down?"

Molly's squirrelly lip gave me more answer than words could. "Molly. That's--oh Hell. What the Hell were you doing?"

"I guess I got worried she'd bolt."

I remembered Molly's insistence that Stephanie be left to her own devices. "And would that have been such a disaster?"

She looked petulant, an expression that didn't sit well on her. "You wanted her to stay."

"Yeah. Stay. Not jailed."

Stephanie was following each comment with a gaze that grew less muddled looking with each sentence. I reached out again, this time slowly, a snake charmer making for a cobra's head.

"I'm sorry, Stephanie. It's just you've got us both spooked."

She stared at me, and Molly made a huffing sound from beneath her knees. Stephanie turned from me to her.

"I had kind of a lot to drink last night," Molly said to her, nonplussed when that tweaked-out stare of her captor's turned on her. "And you're sort of making me sick with your ass on my guts like that."

Stephanie blinked but it was slow, an over-tired, concentrated movement, not the normal rapid fire open and close of someone in the throes of normalcy. She was crashing. She'd probably been crashing when she came over. Now the irritability was taking her. Soon it would be out-and-out sickness. Molly was right: I wasn't ready. We weren't ready. This was none of our business.

"Stephanie," I said and she looked back at me.

I couldn't show her any indecision. "Get off."

There was no movement besides a subtle squirming of Molly's hips. I glared at her: if she was thinking of trying some Ultimate Wrestling move to take Stephanie down, things would definitely go sour. Molly's brow quirked apologetically at me and the squirming stopped.

"You know," she said to Stephanie. "This would look positively *dykish* if someone were to come in right now." She craned her chin downward so it pointed more toward Stephanie's crotch. I expected another outburst of 'fucken dyke' but none came. Instead, Stephanie seemed to do a quick assessment of the situation.

I remembered being in that state at a few points in my life; an assessment meant if I go further I will either get junk or lose my chances of getting junk. Really, it had no more logic to it than that, and I didn't think Stephanie was doing much more than figuring on whether her chances of using would go up or down in the next few minutes.

She must have decided her chances were better if she let Molly up. She rolled over onto the floor and lay there, arms outstretched, chest heaving. Molly rubbed her throat and moved to her side, facing her. Her voice when it came was hoarse, and I realized how tightly Stephanie had been squeezing.

"You know I could have taken you."

Stephanie said nothing. She put her hand on her stomach and rubbed it, then turned to a fetal position, her face toward Molly, who pushed herself to a sitting position.

I reached down to extend her a hand. "You okay?"

Stephanie groaned. I could see that the back of her neck, where her hair stopped and the skin began, was wet.

"Ok," Molly said. "Not so alright." She got to her feet, and hands planted on her hips, surveyed the ball of limbs in front of her. When she spoke again, it was to no one in particular.

"Pretty fucked up, I'd say."

She wiped a hand across her own forehead. Only then did I notice how peaked she looked. The blanched skin was pimpled in spots that I hadn't noticed before. It was as though toxins were pushing their way through her pores and she was fighting off every emergence; that the fight was wearing her out. Great. I had two of them on my hands.

"Why don't you go get a blanket," I told her. "Come on, Stephanie. We'll get you to bed or something."

She groaned from her spot on the floor and I immediately rethought where I'd put her; I didn't think I could deal with soiled sheets and laundry on top of it all. "Maybe not bed, then," I told her. "The couch." I leaned down, hoping my outstretched hand would be clue enough that I wanted her to get up.

She shook her head. "Good," is what she said.

"Good?"

"Good here," she burbled.

"You're good there? Are you sure?" She didn't look good. I didn't really want to think back to my last comedown but the sight of her shoved all kinds of memories into my mind. It had been brutal. I'd ended up wrapped around the toilet bowl with only enough energy to splash the water on my face when I got too hot. I supposed she might not look good where she was but that was about as much as she had in her: to stay there, curled into a ball. I'd done it alone, though, so I knew it was possible. Hideous and dangerous but possible.

Chapter 12

I heard Molly rummaging down the hall in my closet. There were a few expletives, and one or two holy shits, and I imagined she'd found some of my more girlie items that would make her ill to think of putting on: the lacey corset with rhinestones on the boning would certainly put her round the bend. That one was lying out in the open, so I was sure she'd seen it. The feather boas, likewise.

"Stop trying on my crap and get back out here with that blanket," I shouted.

"God, Jay, don't even put that image in my head."

The thunk of something falling on the floor met my ear, and an oops came from the room. I hoped she hadn't dropped my plastic crystal-look heels.

"They're in the closet," I said.

"I am in the closet," she said, annoyed, then I heard her chuckle and mutter to herself.

She made stomping noises as she came back up the hall. Stephanie had taken to rubbing her stomach furiously. There were goose pimples on her arms and she was shivering.

"Hurry up," I said. "I think she's getting worse."

"No doubt," Molly said, and just as she was about to pass me the blanket, someone banged on the door. Molly halted as though her vision had just gone black. She made a slight swaying motion that had me reaching out to her, ready to steady her. She pushed my hand away.

"Your company," is what she said.

"Thank God," I said. "Sherona."

"You might want to get dressed." Molly eyed me up and down, and I realized again that I was still in the creamy silk nightie and housecoat.

I spared a glance for Stephanie who had taken to moaning now, with one foot shaking, tapping sideways against the floor, rerouting the energy, trying to ground it. I felt the saliva fill my own mouth at the remembrance of sickness and want. I felt the sudden need to stop a shivering inside myself. It was almost as though all my cells remembered the pain of detox and needed the complete ravishment of junk.

"Yeah," I said to Molly. "You get the door." I swallowed hard, with one last look at the foot that kept shaking and tapping the floor. I made for the hall and pushed past Molly before she even had a chance to get moving.

"What are you waiting for?" I demanded over my shoulder. It was selfish to make an escape like that but I couldn't stand looking at the tragedy lying on my carpet for one more second. The shriveling of my own skin was making me too damned uncomfortable. I closed the bedroom door behind me when I made it to my room, hearing the sound of the front one being pulled open and Molly saying that I was in the loo doing God knows what in there. I could have strangled her in the instant for giving Sherona a crass image of me.

I needed to put something on. All I had in my bedroom at the moment were masculine clothes. I hadn't yet had a chance to shift the 'closet' items to my bedroom. I pulled out a pair of low-rise bootcuts and yanked a white T-shirt over my head, careful to avoid the stitches at my jawline. The nightie, I stuffed under my pillow. I padded barefoot to the hall.

"Thank God," I said when I saw Sherona, and the out-of-breath sound came out like one big, heaving sigh.

In the dim light of a bar and colored lights of a paving lot's neon sign, Sherona was a beauty; Sherona in the real light of day was breathtaking. Even the female in me could recognize the gorgeousness that was this Amazon queen. I couldn't help stealing a glance at Molly who had gone all agog and tongue-tied. She was at the moment trying to mouth a sentence that was coherent but all it came out as was: Girl sick living room. Well, maybe it wasn't that bad, but you know what memory does to you; it plays tricks and the trick I wanted to remember was of Molly for once being inarticulate in the face of a gorgeous woman.

Despite the wrenching of my stomach and the reality of a very sick girl in the living room and a very I-wasn't-sure-what-was-wrong-with-her dyke in my hallway, I found myself grinning and it felt so good to let something other than anxiety and frustration steal in, even for a few moments that I let it come.

"You got here just in time," I said.

Her analytical eye roved over my frame and landed on the scabbing stitches. "You look better than I thought."

"It appears as though they couldn't beat the freak out of me after all."

She gave me a quizzical look.

"I'm fine," I told her. "It's the girl. The one in the living room."

"Yeah," Molly said. "That's what I said."

Sherona laid a blunt gaze on her. "You said the living room was throwing up a little girl."

Molly looked incredulous and the pallor that had dogged her all morning flushed just a bit. "I did?"

"Pretty much," Sherona said and turned directly to me leaving it apparent she had no time whatsoever to give to Molly.

Sherona moved close enough to me that I could smell the *Chanel* on her. I would have expected something tacky like *Curious* for someone her age, and was pleasantly surprised her scent was something so classic, so appealing. She reached up to touch my jaw but waited, poised just before the electricity of her skin could reach mine. I thought I was holding my breath.

I nodded. "Go ahead. It's okay."

She planted her fleshy part of her palm on the edge of

my jaw and tiptoed her fingers across the cheek to the cut. "No swelling. Bruising's almost gone."

"Hurt like Hell."

"I bet."

She locked eyes with me and I felt a queer revolution somewhere within, the need for junk replaced by something else, something electric. There was a rude sound from my left: Molly, who hated to be ignored.

"Someone should see to the girl throwing up in the living room."

The girl wasn't actually throwing up, but she was still trembling, still curled into a ball. I was relieved to tell you the truth; it meant she might not have taken as much as I'd worried she had.

"Stephanie," I said, kneeling as best I could next to her head. "I've got someone here to see if she can help you out."

There was an almost imperceptible nod. I motioned Sherona to come closer. "She's been blowing all night, I think."

"Blowing?"

"Coke, I think."

"Anything else?"

I nodded, ashamed. "Vikes."

"Holy shit."

"Yeah, well, at least she isn't OD'ing."

"Who says?"

That stopped me. "Well, we just thought--" I looked over at Molly for reinforcement. She clamped her mouth shut. "I guess I figured if she was overdosing, she'd be hemorrhaging from the nose or something. Passing out."

"Maybe," Sherona said. "Maybe not. I'm not sure. I can't remember any of that training." She looked up at me. "What do you think I can do?"

I shrugged. "Help?"

Sherona pulled her plump bottom lip over the top of her teeth and nibbled, thinking, obviously. "I don't know what I can do, J."

I heard the suggestion in the tone: take her to detox, is what it said.

"She doesn't want to go."

"She has to."

Stephanie let out a groan and a few words that sounded like fucken die before I go there.

I looked down at her and put my hand on her shoulder. It felt warm beneath the blanket despite the trembling she was doing. "You just might fucken die if you don't."

She started to cry. The sobs were heart wrenching.

"Don't," I said. "Please don't." I looked up at Sherona. "She's worried she won't get her baby back if they know she's been junking it up."

"I'm sure they know."

"Probably. But no proof. Detox gives that."

"Detox will show she's committed to sobriety."

"We'll lose the kid."

She gave me an odd look and I realized what I'd said.

"She'll lose it," I said as though I'd got it right the first time.

"You don't know that."

Stephanie's sobs came louder; the trembling more rigorous. I heard Molly from behind me. "Listen," she said. "We just need someone to sit with her, get her through."

"Why?" Sherona asked. "You going somewhere?"

"Not really, but what the Hell do we know about drugs and detox."

Sherona surveyed the area: garbage can, blanket, empty cooler bottles, and the dreaded toot I'd made the evening before lying next to the sofa where I'd dropped it. "Quite a lot, apparently."

"It looks like we know more than we do," I lied.

She said nothing, just watched me and I felt my face burn under her gaze.

"This kind of thing always looks bad, Sherona, but it can always be worse."

I thought of how worse it could look. In my early teens, I'd thought hot knifing looked filthy, the epitome of hardcore using. I caught an echo of something from those same teens: hoarse taunts of freak and gayboy; I smelled cigarettes and the stink of burning flesh and my mind reeled to how worse 'this kind of thing' could look: brown liquid in borrowed spoons mixed with grubby gas station restroom water. Blood stained needles poking into yellowed veins. Blackened meth pipes sucking up plumes of gritty smoke from a crackled piece of tin foil. Bad visions, yes, all in the name of making worse images disappear. So yeah, oh Hell, yeah, it could look a lot worse.

The one image that didn't look bad to me in my memory was of that baby in its green blanket. I clung to it, that picture, so hard it could have been a photo in my hands.

"She's my next door neighbor," I said of Stephanie.

Sherona nodded. "Sure," is all she said before she aimed her attentions to the scrawny user on the floor. "Stephanie, is it?" she asked kindly. "I'm just going to sit with you. Are you in pain?"

Stephanie attempted a nod. "Sick."

"How long?"

I answered. "Since nine at least. I'm not sure how much she had before, but none since then." I looked at Molly. "None, right?"

She shrugged. "Don't think so."

Sherona closed her eyes, her hands fleeting across Stephanie's exposed skin from forearm to forehead. "I think we should call 911."

Stephanie yelped and made an attempt to get up that resulted in her collapse again, flat on her back, chest heaving. Sherona had her palm on her chest maybe to hold her down, maybe to calm her.

"You're sick," she soothed. "I don't think we can help you by ourselves." She looked at me. "Do you have any Vitamin Water? Gatorade? Anything like that. I think she needs some electrolytes or something. Definitely some kind of nutrients. I don't think plain water would be easy on her stomach, but the more we can get in her, the more we can flush."

I mentally ran through my fridge. I didn't buy Vitamin Water or Gatorade, but I had some Crystal Lite in there all mixed up. And I had root beer Popsicles.

"Not sure about the ice yet. Can you warm up the juice?" she said.

"Sure, just pour in a bit of warm water."

"Yeah, yeah, that'd be fine. Room temperature. Body temperature would be better. You have a thermometer?"

I shook my head and watched as she furrowed her brow, thinking. "Then just test it on your wrist like with formula."

I heard a snork come from Molly's corner. "Need a bottle too?" she said.

I gave her a dirty look. "This isn't the time, Molly."

Sherona waved away my annoyance. "No, no," she said. "That's not a bad idea."

"A bottle."

"Not a bottle, a sippy cup. You think she had one for the baby?"

I made a half-decent attempt to kneel so Stephanie could hear me. "The baby have a sippy cup yet?"

She shook her head and managed a few tremulous words. "Maybe one from the baby shower. In her bedroom. Closet."

I looked at Molly, half relieved to have an excuse to get out of there, half afraid of what we'd see when we went next door. "Come with me?"

"Hell, yeah."

I crammed my feet into a pair of old running shoes, heel still sticking out until I could shove a finger in the back to yank them up. It must have been comical to Molly who snorted again. "Now you're just milking it,"

"What?" I said. "I'm still sore."

"Mmmmm. Indeed," she answered, but she held onto my hips so I could balance as I pulled on the sneaker backs. She bent to adjust the rim so it wasn't crooked. "Better?"

I nodded and she let go a huff. "This isn't going to be pretty."

She opened my apartment door and held it so I could go ahead of her into the next. I went straight down Stephanie's hall, letting my vision kind of tunnel out. I didn't want to see what was in there. Didn't want to smell the smells. I just headed to where I thought would be my bedroom if it was my apartment--the place I knew from early morning wakings, where the baby slept. I flicked on the light.

"Holy shit," Molly said.

I turned to where she stood just behind me, and couldn't help my own expletive. "Fuck."

"Fuck indeed."

Chapter 13

The light had flooded the small room with what might as well have been pure Divinity. I'm not sure what Molly expected; I know what I expected, but it seemed neither of us was prepared for the baby's room as it stood.

The crib was neatly made up with a fluffy pink blanket; the bumper pads were a matching hue with rollicking cartoon bunnies. Above the crib swayed a mobile with Winnie the Pooh characters. It was mismatched, sure, but it was obviously well cared for. I stepped closer and could smell fabric softener and Ivory Snow. There was a stack of baby soap on the little bureau that sent out a baby fresh scent. Next to the stack sat a package of diapers and jars of Vaseline. I pulled open a drawer.

"Holy shit," I said.

"What?"

"Neat freak," I said and Molly crept close to peek over my shoulder.

"It's perfect."

"It all is," I said. What we had stepped into had been a miniature sanctuary for that baby. Maybe it was true, what Stephanie had said: She did try. She was a good mother--or at least, as good as she knew how to be.

"Check the closet," Molly said.

I didn't care now what the rest of the house looked like; I'd seen enough to tell me Stephanie did care about her little bundle. Maybe she just needed help. I felt reinvigorated. If I couldn't help, I'd find someone who could. I had fuzzy images of the infant swaddled in fleece blankets, cooing happily, chubby fingers clenched around my thumb. Thriving.

"Here's a sippy cup." I pulled a purple plastic cup with Dora the Explorer running across its surface brandishing a backpack.

"Shame," I said, looking around the room at the perfect neatness that contrasted so perfectly with the chaos I knew was in the living room and kitchen.

There was a small photo frame on the bureau with a picture of the newborn taken moments after birth--the kind of thing hospitals take where the noses are all squashed and the skin is flushed with effort. I stared at it for long moments till Molly spoke and broke my focus.

"Not a shame," Molly said. "It's not real, Jay."

"Not real? Come on. This room is perfect."

Molly ran blunt fingers through her dregs of black and white tipped hair. "It's an illusion. What's real to that girl is the junk. That's it. You know that."

I couldn't help touching the fairy night light next to the crib. "I might know it, but I can't believe it."

"Suit yourself; you'll be in for a Hell of a ride. Her kind doesn't get better."

"Her kind? What the Hell's that supposed to mean?" I watched as her expression shifted in front of me, and I realized she was testing me. Again. How many times would I have to write the damn thing?

"I've been clean, you know I have." I was surprised to hear my voice, as low as it was, almost a whisper. I expected it to sound angry not simpering. I closed my eyes to the sound of my own voice, shutting her out for an instant, hoping she'd respond that yes, yes, she did know I was clean, and hoping against hope at the same time that she'd say nothing at all.

She'd been with me the night I'd used last.

It's not like I wanted to end my life that night with a tomato knife. Not at all; who would ever make a decision like that. It's just that it had been the only thing I could find in her kitchen with an edge that was clean. It sounds stupid now, the thought that the knife that would kill you would need to be free of debris, but I never questioned it then. But it's weird, the way your mind works when you're high. One minute you're laughing with a buddy, sharing stories of conquests and failures, of drunken nights and hilariously bad trips. The next your mind is so focused it hurts as bad as a super-clear sinus. Reality gets all befuddled in the weight of the light that's shed on it.

I'd left her in her living room while I went to the kitchen for a glass of water, thinking I could slake the thirst that had come on after a two-day drug binge. We'd been out of junk for about three hours, which meant the beast within was stretching awake in ways that made my throat tight. I was tired. Exhausted, really. The medicine just wasn't working its magic anymore, and I couldn't truly get a stronger scrip than I was already taking. So I grabbed the blade from the drawer. Stuffed it in my jacket, thinking I should at least have the decency to leave her apartment. A good friend wouldn't leave that kind of mess. Besides, I didn't want her to save me, after all. I just knew it was over.

I was giddy. Eager. I said my goodbyes hastily, shaking her hand as though I'd just met her at a job interview. She gave me an odd glance, squeezed and pumped my hand all while I said things like: had a great time. The best. You're the best, Molly. God. I hope you find yourself a good woman one of these days. Then I pulled my coat tighter so I could zipper it against the cold and was out the door. I felt as though I'd injected helium into my veins. I was leaning against a graffitied wall two blocks away, legs splayed out in front of me before I noticed I hadn't pulled on my shoes when I'd left and was still in the slippers I kept at her place.

She found me of course. Gurgling like a baby on Gottingen Street where the prostitutes trolled the cobbled sidewalks. I don't think I'd felt the blade against my skin; I don't remember it. I only remember her hands coming at me through the dark, the pressing of her palms against my throat.

"Jesus," she'd said, her voice barely registering as anything more than the breeze that blows up from the harbor. A streetlight made a halo around her head. My guardian angel.

"Jesus," she said again now as we stood in the baby's room.

I adjusted my brain to take in the spotless bedroom, the fairy nightlight and let go the dankness of the alley. "I'm clean," I said to her again.

Molly wouldn't look me in the eye. She fiddled the light switch up and down. "I know," she said, deciding finally to leave the light off. Sunshine crept in through the gauze curtains. It seemed ethereal in there, the Winnie the Pooh, the Dora the Explorer, the fantasy fairies sprinkled all around. Maybe it was an illusion. And here we both were in it, Molly and I.

"You okay?" I asked her, knowing it was the same thing she was wanting to ask me.

She sighed. "Been better."

I noticed, now the light was off, that she did look kind of gray, so I'd been right earlier. "You're not sleeping."

She shook her head. "Not for 52 hours anyway. Well, 52 and a bit, not counting the quick blackout when I hit the floor with Miss Thing in there."

"And here I've been keeping you up."

She lifted a shoulder. "I wouldn't be able to go out of it even if you plied me with sleeping pills." She tried on a grin that made her face look like a grimacing pumpkin. The expression flattened out in seconds. "But don't. I don't think I could take it at the moment."

"I'd never."

"Never say never, my friend." She reached for the sippy cup, ready to move on, it seemed. She threw it into the air when she'd taken it from me, then caught it with her right fist. "Come on. Let's get this over to that gorgeous gal."

I hung behind just long enough to grab the photo from

the bureau and tucked it beneath my armpit. I didn't know why I needed it, but I did.

When I think about it, I don't believe we were gone more than ten minutes, but I suppose that's sufficient time for an ambulance to make it across town. Molly and I closed the door to Stephanie's apartment when they brushed past us. They weren't on the rush, just pulled out a stretcher from the back and proceeded matter-of-factly up the front steps. The first paramedic yanked open the door, able to balance his end of the stretcher while doing so.

I felt a weird sense of relief.

"Down this way," I said to him.

Sherona met me in the hall. "Sorry, J. I had to."

I patted her shoulder. "I know. Thanks."

With less kerfuffle than I'd thought, Stephanie was onto the stretcher and out the door into the back of the ambulance. "I suppose they'll know what to do," I said.

"Course they will," Sherona said. "She wasn't overdosing, I don't think; or if she had, she managed to hold it off. She has pains in her chest, though. She probably did some damage."

I nodded, mute.

"They'll help her."

"Sure," I said.

I felt the frame under my arm and squeezed so I could feel the corner of it sticking into my rib. It's okay, girl, I told the frame and the newborn within it. We'll be okay.

Chapter 14

After the paramedics left, we had the long discussion about what we, if anything, were going to do next. In the end, we decided that we'd set about clearing up Stephanie's apartment for her so that when she came home from detox in a week or so she would have a clean start. By this time it was about four in the afternoon and Molly was winding down enough that it looked like she could sleep. I sent her into my bedroom with the explicit directions that she was not to go rifling through my drawers.

"What makes you think I'd want to ruffle through your crap?"

I thought of the time I'd caught her trying on my men's boxer briefs over top her jeans. "You know why."

She harrumphed. "Sheesh, get curious once and never live it down."

Sherona looked confused at the exchange.

"Molly doesn't get me," I said by way of explaining. I wanted to bask in the notion that for now, regardless of what gender I thought I might be, she had accepted me and didn't want to go further into shoddy detail.

To my surprise, Sherona didn't question; she touched my hand instead as she sat next to me, crossed the right leg over the left knee and leaned back into the sofa cushions. It had been an exhausting morning and afternoon. I reveled in the feel of someone next to me, the heat that comes off a body that's worked, the smell of a person's skin. Molly took one look at the coziness of us two and announced she would indeed try to settle into a good sleep.

"Don't wake me unless the Almighty has pulled his sword out and is ready to do battle."

"That Pentecostal shit has warped your brain," I told her.

"Beats being ignorant." She didn't sashay to my room so much as swagger. I heard her grumble about the bed not being made then nothing more came from the room except a groan as though she'd just discovered she'd survived said Apocalypse.

I too leaned back onto the sofa, reveling in the feel of Sherona's palm on my leg. It was warm and comforting. "Thanks," I said to her. I wanted to say more but how does a person go into an explanation like the morning would entail? Thanks just about summed it up as best as I could.

She mumbled a 'no problem' back at me and blew out an exhausted sigh.

"She's quite a number," Sherona said.

"I guess I wasn't thinking about how hard she'd be to dial in," I answered, remembering the manic strength of Stephanie's grip.

"I thought you knew each other well."

"Nope. Just met her yesterday." I said it under my breath almost as the realization hit me that it did seem odd that a stranger would go to such lengths to help out another. Is that what true compassion really was? To aid without thought for reward. I thought of Stephanie's daughter and realized that had been my motivation. So maybe it wasn't compassion, but selfishness after all. I didn't feel so good about that.

"J?"

I turned to her grin. "Yeah?"

"I'm talking about Molly."

"Oh." Molly. Of course. I should have understood right away by the very nature of my best friend that she'd leave an impression; she always did. I felt even worse then. "She is indeed a number; 666 if I counted correctly." I faked a chuckle, aware that it didn't even sound the least bit genuine.

She seemed to be waiting for something, more words, perhaps, on the type of person Molly was. She must have succumbed to Molly's charm after all, without my realizing the allure had reared its head. I sighed within and set out to offer Sherona what I thought she wanted: history, some sort of wiggle room to scooch into when the opportunity arose. It wouldn't need to--Molly would make the space.

"She's complicated."

"I imagine."

"We've been through a lot together." I thought of the first time I'd met Molly although 'meet' wasn't exactly the right description for the event. I'd been wrapped around the cold bowl of a ladies restroom toilet, shivering with my shirt half off and my pants around my ankles. A needle still hanging from my arm. I'd heard the raucous of the gay bar music and telltale noises of the debauchery come and go as the bathroom door opened and closed.

"Yup," I said to Sherona. "We go way back some three years or more."

"A lot can happen in three years."

I got a quick vision of Molly's boots before I knew they belonged to Molly. They'd entered the stall next to me; I could see the thickness of the sole as they backed into the toilet in their stall. Pissing. Toilet tissue spinning. Flushing. Then...waiting.

I'd squeezed my eyes shut then, thinking surely she'd see the puddle of brown on the floor next to me. Hell, she'd probably smelled the shit when she came in. I tried to keep the groan of shame quiet even as the groan of sickness took my breath. The cramps waged battle with the high and the high waged battle with the despair that I'd once again come into a wrong bathroom. Why the Hell would a gay bar have separate, labeled bathrooms anyway?

"J?" Sherona's voice sent a ripple through the memory.

I looked at her, trying to see her distinct features in the dark, to remind me where I was.

"You went off somewhere."

"Yeah, I know."

"Bad place?"

"No, not really," I said. "Just a puddle of shit and a bad trip, is all."

"And that's not bad."

I shrugged, though she couldn't see it in the dark. "The night I met Molly."

"Ah, so it couldn't be all bad, then. Right?"

"Molly is a lot of things, Sherona, but bad is not one of them."

"I see," she said.

I wanted to stop talking. I didn't really want to reinforce the Molly-allure any more than I had to, but it was all true. Molly was my angel in disguise. And she could care less if her wings had been clipped by her maker.

"I love her," I said. "She's good people."

Good people described Molly the way food described chocolate. I thought of the way she'd leaned down onto the floor, sticking her face in my stall and took one look at me and my shivering, retching, shitting mess and crawled under to get me. She unlocked the door, pulled my jeans up my legs and dragged me to the sink to help me wash up. I'd been too high to do anything by then but hang on the sink and drool. I vaguely remembered her growl at the bouncers for waving their hands in front of their noses as she strong-armed me from the bathroom, imagined she'd paid the cabbie. I came around on a sofa to her laying cold, wet cloths on my forehead. Good people could be a decent description if you spoke a different language. Who cares what our friendship contained after that?

I'd keep all of that to myself, though, thank you. To describe Molly would be to describe myself. I just didn't want Sherona to see that me in comparison to the me who could help an unknown neighbor.

"She does sound wonderful."

"Yes," I said, unable to keep the self-loathing out of my own voice. "Molly is a way better person than I am." I pushed deeper into the couch, letting silence hide what couldn't be secreted away by the darkness and she seemed to accept it; she said nothing in response, just placed her hand on my thigh and squeezed gently.

I let her sit; if she'd indeed come off a ten-hour shift like she'd said on the phone, she was probably doubly fatigued now. I felt a stitch in my side where I'd obviously labored with rapid breathing under the stress of the morning. I let my breathing fall into rhythm with hers. Soon enough, I think we were all asleep. I had dreams of casting a net into a froth of sea and coming out with hermaphrodite fish with no eyes.

There was a blackness to the dream that stole my wind, and the sense of being trapped and tangled in a net scared me awake. I opened my eyes to a darkened room and the feel of a mouth against mine. It took me a moment to adjust from dream to reality, and in the panicked attempt, I pushed at the weight that was on top of me.

"Shhh," came the soothing response. "Shh. It's just me."

I wanted to ask what she was doing, but it was abundantly clear by the way she was fumbling in the dark with the button on my jeans. I made a feeble attempt to pry her fingers off my zipper.

"It's okay," she whispered. "She's asleep."

I gathered that she thought for some reason I'd care what Molly thought. "No," I said. "No, it's not Molly. We're not like that."

"You're not---involved?"

I chuckled. "Not even remotely."

I felt her mumbling "good" against my neck. Her breath was a moist welcoming breeze there, lighting a million minute flames down the small of my back. I wasn't sure how I was going to handle this. A week ago, I'd have wanted nothing more than exactly what she was doing right now: namely, cupping my balls in a way that made them stretch against the fabric of my underwear.

"Sherona, I--"

I felt rather than saw her sit back against the couch. The hairs around my testicles prickled, then allowed the cold air to tighten the skin.

"You don't want to," she said flatly, but there was more in her tone, a sense of disappointment, yes, but also of humiliation.

"Well, it's not as if I wouldn't," I started. How to explain, how to go there? I mean, despite all appearances, I was supposed to be, right at this moment, femme. Straight femme despite the tingling of my prick that said it wanted sex.

"It's Molly, isn't it?"

I couldn't lie. "It's not Molly, but it's not you, either." I couldn't believe I'd misread her about Molly. I was both relieved and afraid. "It's me."

She snorted in the dark, "I've heard that one before."

The distance between us seemed to grow. I wanted to pull her closer, stroke her hair, ease the pain I knew she must be feeling. And there was more, I knew it, deep inside, but I couldn't name it. Instead, I reached for words.

"Sherona, I'm not what you think I am."

"I know you're an addict. I know you're hurt. I know you're hurting."

"All true."

"Yeah, well." She was pulling away emotionally. Building a wall. Cementing it. Getting ready to walk away.

"I like you, Sherona. I do. I really do. "There's something about you--"

"About me, I know," she said, and I realized it had come out terribly. She was taking it wrong.

"No," I protested. "Not about you, about us. Something I can't explain,"

I could sense her nod in the semi-dark. "Yeah, something," she said, but it was an agreement and not an invitation. The wall was curing, I could almost smell it hardening.

"There is something, Sherona. Another time, maybe."

"Yup, I've heard that one, too."

I had to dive in, it seemed. There'd be no easy way out of this with my dignity. And here I thought I'd be able to avoid having her know my nitty gritty--at least for a while yet.

"Sherona, I'm a woman." There it was as bald as a newborn rat.

"Well, I can't say I've heard that one."

I could almost feel her getting up off the sofa, thinking I was lying, making up some horrible thing to piss her off and get her out of my hair. Another moment, and she would be up, and out, and then I'd never get to see her. Maybe ever again. A woman scorned. A woman beautiful and robust as this one. I'd be lucky if she even left without hitting me.

I reached out, hoping there'd be a hand on the other end, hoping she'd take mine. I waggled my fingers, inched closer, feeling that if she didn't respond, I'd have to try again. For some reason, for some unexplainable reason, I wanted to touch her. I felt her knee against my palm. She'd made a barrier with her body, one I'd have to break down as gently as I could if I wanted to keep the peace between us.

"Please," I said and the begging note in my tone didn't surprise me.

I wanted her to stay. I wanted her in my life; I realized that. I wanted, oh Hell, a week ago I wanted her the same as I did now. Why couldn't I admit it to myself? I wanted to be asexual in that moment. I wanted to be male or female or both if that's what would keep her there, and I had a hard time deciding whether it was because I wanted something within her, or her very being, or her sex. It was all mingled together in such odd ways that I couldn't really say I wasn't gay in that moment. Neither could I say I was heterosexual. It didn't matter to me what gender she was. Her sex, her being, her body parts just did not matter. The musk beneath the Chanel fragrance she wore, scenting of heat and unfathomable pulses.

Her kindness, that thing within her that brought her unquestioning to my home. I wanted it.

I wanted it all.

I let my palm lay on her knee, and the warmth of her skin moved through me. Moving in small circles even as I spoke in a whisper. "Don't go," I said. "I'm not doing this right."

She leaned forward; her fingers touched my chin, gripping it beneath. "I won't go."

And then her mouth was on mine again, covering mine, her tongue exploring the depth and width of it, teasing my teeth and palette. There was the heady taste of brandy and citrus, as though she'd decompressed after her shift with a snifter of cognac and Grand Marnier and it lingered in her pores like she was lingering over my lips. It wasn't a demanding kiss. It was languid. She made me feel each movement of her mouth in detail, like the undulations of a serpent wriggling its way out of a skin too tight, and I couldn't do much but imagine her body moving the same way over me, covering me and demanding in a quiet manner, all I had to give her.

I knew I was hard. I knew I wanted her.

It took all the energy within me to pull away, and even in her withdrawal, she was lazy. It seemed she imagined she had all eternity to complete each moment, each movement.

"There is something between us," she admitted.

The conversation was going in reverse and I felt giddy. Almost drunk. "Yeah. I know."

She moved closer. Her legs had stretched behind her enough that she could lean forward onto me if she wanted, or push herself up and away if she didn't. I supposed it all had to do with what I decided. Still, I had to be honest.

"I really am a woman," I said. "You'd be having sex with another woman. You need to know that."

"Are you really?"

"Yes."

"And you're straight as a woman?"

"Yes."

I heard her sigh in thought. I wasn't sure what she was thinking; she'd cupped my balls earlier, so she knew my natal physique. Could she make the leap to core physique? I couldn't know. I was only certain it would be difficult for her to process: my body and my gender were at odds for her, this much was sure by the way she touched me again, almost tentatively, as though to seek out again what she'd known earlier. She saw me as a man. I presented as a man; she wanted sex with a man. Would it matter to her that the body and the gender were not the same. To me it meant she was crossing the line from heterosexuality to bisexuality; I wondered if it meant the same to her. And it mattered to me what it meant to her. I couldn't have her if she didn't understand. But I couldn't make a sound. Couldn't speak. This line needed to be crossed with her consent, not coercion.

It seemed there was little time from the sigh she exhaled and the movement she made that had her body covering mine. She was weighty in a way that felt delirious, as though a comforter had been lain across me as I lay freezing and alone in a tundra. It stole my breath, leaving me in an oxygen-starved delirium. There was no panic in the weight, only a sense that though I could barely move, when I did, my muscles would work their way through molasses and honey. Then the undulations began as I knew they would. The serpent in her, her tongue, her body crept across me, the length of me, exploring every inch, peeling away the layers and leaving me naked to the air, to her inspection.

What she did, she did well. Where she touched me, she touched me perfectly. She left no wrinkle of skin unsmoothed. There was an uncertain moment where she paused, lingering over my chest. Her breath felt hot against the scars there, and then, almost like a headlong swimmer jumping off a diving board, she plunged.

I felt her lips graze the scars on my ribcage, her fingers

trace the sliver of leftover self-inflicted panic on my throat. She said nothing when she touched these, merely grunted at the raised feel of each on her finger or her lips as she met them. I had the sense that they were disappearing as she traced the silver lines, that with each millimeter of touch, they dissipated like steam into the air and evaporated into nothingness.

There was movement inside my chest that had nothing to do with the air I took in or the pump that pushed it through my body. Every lick of her tongue set my skin to fever. Each time she kissed my skin I felt as though my chest became more buoyant, that it could lift me into the air like a helium balloon and that I'd sail thus, extended into the atmosphere. I wondered if this was how angels felt or if this was what they'd fallen from grace for.

And when I could stand it no more, she straddled me and rode slowly, deliciously. I saw her breasts, those large, fulsome and shadowed teardrops sway before me. I would have them in my mouth, I would feel them in my palms, and even as I thought it, they were there in my hands, against my lips. I rose so I could press my entire body against hers, feel the sweat on her skin, allow the grease of our bodies to slide against each other. We moved in near unison, and it was the awkward mismatched step that drove me on.

My heart was a ragged tattered thing, pounding in my chest. The sheen of sweat and saliva made my skin vulnerable to the cold. Still, I didn't want to move, to break the spell. I lay on the sofa with her stretched out beside me in the cranny of the backrest and cushions. She was tall enough that her toes could tickle the sole of my foot even as she licked the tip of my chin. I felt like I'd never felt before. I thought at that moment that God and Satan could easily be chattering together over a cup of tea and a few cookies.

The darkness grew humid as we lay there together allowing the combined heat of our bodies to create a blanket of hot moist air. I think I fell asleep within moments, but on the verge of tipping into the abyss, I believed I could hear her whispering to me. The specter of sleep kept me from being able to reply to the words that crept into my subconscious, the wonderment of what exactly we had done to each other.

I woke to the sound of birds and a hefty weight on my side: the scratchiness of the textile on my neck told me it was the Hudson's Bay blanket from the hall linen closet. It seemed Sherona had gone and I'd slumped onto my left shoulder in a stupor. She must have rummaged for a blanket before heading out the door, bless her heart. The puddle of drool beneath my cheek had sopped into the sofa cushion and gone clammy.

I eased myself off the couch, running my hand across the dampened spot to see how big it was. I'd been completely out by the size of it, and out for a good long time. I stumbled into the kitchen so I could grab a peek at the oven clock: 6:30 a.m. Well, it hadn't been quite enough sleep in light of all the goings-on, but I was wide-awake now, and there was nothing for that even if I wanted to sleep for days.

Thoughts of sleeping for a few days reminded me that Molly was in my room. I wondered what had truly brought her home and to me in particular. I got up, stepping on the condom wrapper, where it stuck to my foot and had to be pulled off. I yanked on my jeans and T-shirt, tiptoed down the hall to my room and listened at the door with my ear pressed against the laminated wood. All was quiet. I checked the front door for her shoes. Still there. So I wasn't alone. Good. For some reason, I didn't want to be.

I padded back to the kitchen to schedule some coffee with my percolator. The titty mug still rested on the counter. I ran it under water from the tap and gave the rim a scrub with soap. I left it clean on the sideboard in easy reach for when Molly decided to get up.

With coffee set to brew in an hour, I shuffled into my closet to begin the process of sorting through the items that would navigate to my bedroom and the ones that would get shoved further back in now I'd shifted completely into the femme me. The sex of the night before could have been a dream; it had that slow sense of unreality to it that made me doubt it happened. Nothing felt real, not the cold feel of the floor on my feet nor the riot of materials and colors that met me when I opened the door. I wasn't sure if it was the fog of oversleep or the haze of confusion after all the events of the last couple days, or even the stupid sense of knowing but not knowing if I'd had sex a few hours earlier, but I couldn't for the life of me figure out where to start.

I picked up the photo of Stephanie's baby from where I'd put it on my bureau. Her skin was fuzzy in the photo, red and crinkled. Her eyes were crossed, trying to focus at whatever light was trying to ignite the photo into being. I put it back on the bureau, placing it so it faced the window, and I turned to survey the space.

There was the metal rack of bras and costume lingerie that stood against the shortest wall near the door, its stainless aluminum blinking in the light of rising sun coming through the curtains. I wasn't sure what I should do with that: I didn't have a lover--regular lover, at least--at the moment, so the costumes would be useless to move, and the bras, despite how pretty many of them were, just didn't seem right for some reason. I had a stack of shoes in every height and every heel thickness. They were neatly propped against the railing of the shoe stand. I thought of the comfort of my Converse and looked down at my feet. The big toe of each was wide and blunt with a bunion on the outmost edge from wearing delicate and pointed shoes during my femme stages. I rubbed at one with the sole of my other foot. Bastards made an otherwise attractive foot look distorted and ugly: the price of beauty, I supposed. I took a look around; this was all the price of beauty, really. I spared a thought for all the money I'd put into swapping genders to match my mood. How fruitless it seemed to me now.

I moved to the wall with the window. I had three bureaus and bureau-like pieces of furniture there, filled with skirts and lacy tops as well as drawers of underwear. As I rummaged through a few, I realized how compulsive a shopper I could be. Dollar store panties lay beside expensive specialty shop thongs. You can imagine the thongs, I'm sure: the string up the backside wasn't a big deal-- any person can fit a piece of floss between the old butt cheeks. The front panel? Well, now, that posed a problem, and despite my compulsion for sleazy thongs, I had never worn a pair. I just couldn't and had never been able to find a way to stuff my junk into the small triangle of front material. The fact that I had them, drew a confession about self-medication that lips could never make.

I made a harrumphing sound at the realization and pushed the drawer closed, disgruntled.

Lastly there were the four mannequins I'd scabbed from one of my places of employment in the city: a clothing store for big and tall women. All but one--that sported a pink boa-- was naked at the moment, but I used them in my femme state to put outfits together before I went out on the town: one was for lingerie with matching bra and panties, one was for the first layer of dress, one for the blazer, shoes, and matching accessories, and the final was for the outer layer. I always wanted to see how each layer looked separately as well as how it coordinated. They took up a lot of space, actually. And they were all ugly. Not petite and feminine the way I believed femme felt. In fact, they looked decidedly unlike what I felt. Why had I stolen them in the first place? They might fit my proportions, but they certainly didn't fit my psyche.

And so it was that I was paralyzed by what was in that closet and what it meant. I smelled the aroma of coffee long before I realized I'd been in there for an hour and had done absolutely nothing. An hour had gone by, then, and I was no further ahead than when I'd started. To Hell with it. Maybe it just wasn't time to pass judgment on what I should be wearing. I'd been too hasty in my assessment of being femme. In fact, the jeans I had on didn't necessarily feel wrong. The T-shirt wasn't truly a horrible item of clothing. I felt comfortable enough. It didn't make sense: If I was femme, I should feel differently. I should think differently. Yet, I didn't feel different. I just felt like me.

I made my way down the hall into the kitchen and aimed straight for the coffee. It looked pale in the carafe, not deep, earthy brown like it should have, but a pale kind of pekoe tea color. Shit. I must have, in my befuddled state, put too little grounds in for the water I'd added. Waste of good coffee and energy, really, to have done something so stupid. I stared at the pot feeling a certain sense that I couldn't name. All I knew was I wanted to pick up the pot and throw it into the sink.

I settled for swearing. One or two rounds of a few select curses like the F-bomb and the C-word. Both felt very nice on my tongue and decidedly filthy. I ended up chewing on the inside of my cheek because it did sound awfully weird to hear a litany of *fuck fuck fuck cunt fuck cunt* for a few minutes.

"Well, now," a voice drawled from behind me. "I do so love that word. Both of them actually, even better when they're spoken together like that."

Molly looked rested at least, but not better. Her hair was a bunch of flat gobs against her skull. There was salty residue on her cheek where she'd obviously drooled out her fatigue.

She inclined her head to the counter where the pot still waited, saved from its down-the-sink fate. "That coffee?" she asked, rubbing her eyes.

"Sort of."

"Sort of is good enough for me." She ran her fingers under the cold tap and scrubbed at her eyes and corners of her mouth. She went to the counter where I'd left her favorite mug. The pot got upended and caramel colored liquid streamed and disappeared behind the boobs. "You still got cream?"

"You can't possibly add cream to that shit."

"What? I like cream."

"But it's already weak."

"So?"

I flipped my hand over my head. What did I care if she wanted to weaken urine-colored java anyway. I jammed at the button to shut off the percolator.

"Someone's cranky."

I glared at her. "I'm not cranky."

"You get your period or something?"

I didn't find that funny, and I wasn't about to grace the stupidity of the comment with anything other than a flat back. I went to the fridge to find something to eat. I hoped the dregs of food I'd managed to pick up a week or so ago were still good. I'd not been out grocery shopping since forever. There were eggs in there. Some cheese that would add to an omelet just fine when I cut off the mold. I found a package of tortillas that I could wrap it all in.

Molly put her arm over my shoulder, peering in from beside me.

"Omelets?"

I nodded and she stretched, her lean arms snaking into the air over her head. Satisfied she'd milked every bit of muscle tension and release she could, she nicked in past me and grabbed the short container of blend.

"I'll be right back," she said and left it on the counter next to her mug. She sauntered down the hall and back into my bedroom where she closed the door. Maybe she planned to change or something. I poured a small amount of cream into her coffee and put the blend back in the fridge, retreating with the carton of eggs and the package of moldy and edge-hardened cheddar. It was hard to explain even to myself how I felt this morning. Ragged, maybe. Like the cheese: palatable, but just not quite right.

Despite the hours of sleep, I felt tiredness creep between my shoulder blades.

I heard the click of my bedroom door as I broke up the eggs and filled a wide-mouthed bowl. Molly was back in the kitchen, unchanged as I was scrambling up the half dozen eggs. "Cut the gunk of that cheese, will ya?" I said to her. "But wash your hands first. God only knows where they've been the last few hours."

"Oh, very funny," she said. "What do you want me to do with this?"

Without breaking beating stride, I looked up at her to see her holding out a small plastic baggie with a glop of powder at the bottom right corner. "Oh Hell no," I said.

"I'm afraid yes," she answered, managing to look ashamed and cocky all at the same time.

"Molly, what the Hell?"

She shrugged. "I guess you could say I got a problem."

For the first time that morning, I really looked at her. Her eyes glistened and there was a flush to her cheeks that I realized, just then, had come and gone intermittently during her brief visit.

"I don't need this." I dropped the fork onto the counter and it clacked into the dish.

She quirked her brow apologetically. "I'm so sorry, Jay. I'm afraid that's not the worst of it."

I backed away, palms in front of me, defensive, warding off evil. No. This wasn't happening. It wasn't. She'd just have to get the Hell out if it was hers. It wasn't hers though. Please God, let it not be hers. "It's Stephanie's, right?"

I waited for her to answer, you know I did. You also can imagine my sense of desperation right then. After the last days, the last hours. Really. I mean, would you believe this shit if I wasn't telling you so? It sounds made up, doesn't it?

"Molly?" I felt the table corner against my back. "It's Stephanie's right? You found it when we were over there?"

She dropped the baggie onto the counter and picked up the fork to run it through the eggs in the dish. I watched a stream of milky yellow and a glistening lump of translucent white run across the tines back into the dish. "I did find some over there."

I felt my shoulders relax just a hair. Okay. This didn't

have to be as bad as I thought. I was just being pessimistic; can you blame me, though? It had been a Hell of a week.

"But this one's mine," she said and nudged the bag toward me with the flat of the fork. It left a slime of egg on the plastic.

"Yours?"

"Uh huh."

"And what is it you want me to say about that?"

She shrugged.

"I mean," I said. "You picked just this moment to tell me? After the day we had yesterday?"

"Yesterday would have been better to tell you?"

"No, you fucking dyke, yesterday would not have been better."

"Well, what, then? What?" She grabbed at the bowl of mix and dumped it in the frying pan I'd put on the stove. No butter. No heat. Just dumped it in.

"And don't call me a dyke. I hate that word." She was sullen. The way she stared down into the egg mixture, watching it begin to bubble in the middle was evidence of that; normally, she'd step aside and expect me to do my culinary magic. She poked at a rising bubble with the tip of her finger.

"You can't do that," I said.

"The fuck I can't."

I stepped closer so I could grab a spatula from the drawer next to the stove and twisted the knob onto lower heat. "You need to cover it, not pop it." I eased her aside. "So what's the whole story, anyway?" I moved the frying pan off the element so I could have time to grate some of the cheese before it was done cooking.

She passed me the block and a grater. "You don't want to know so why should I tell you?"

"I want to know. You know I do. But Hell, did you expect anything less than how I reacted?"

"I'm in a mess. I didn't know how else to say it. I would have told you yesterday--"

"Yesterday was a bad day--"

"Hello? I was there, remember?" She watched me as I jammed the block of cheese over the grater with a tad too much gusto. "Um," she said. "You left the mold on."

"Damn."

"It's okay," she said. "I'll just pick those bits out for you." She took the bowl from me and rummaged, picking out threads with bits of green and black on them.

"You know what?" she said after a couple of minutes, then put the bowl on the counter. "I don't need cheese in mine. Let's just have scrambled."

It was as good an idea as we'd had in two days. I jammed the frying pan back on the heat and with a rubber spatula, broke up the mixture into lumps where the egg hadn't solidified, and flat chunks where it had. Neither of us said anything more til we had plates in hand and went to the stoop where the cool breeze coming up across the road relieved the pressure of a conversation gone bad and the sun peeking over the houses painted the step with orangey light.

"I'm sorry," I said, scooping a curd into my mouth with my fingers. I'd left the forks behind in the kitchen, eager to leave the kitchen and the baggie on the counter where I wouldn't have to think about it.

She balanced her plate on her knees. "Yeah, me too."

"We're really not well-suited to be friends, I don't think."

"Gawd, no. We suck."

I chuckled. "You're an idiot and I'm a short-tempered jerk."

"Bitch," she corrected.

"Fucking bitch," I added, appreciating that she'd remembered.

"Drama queen."

"That too."

"Freak."

"Well, that's both of us."

"Damn straight." She brought her plate to her mouth and sucked in a couple of dregs from the edge. An early morning motorist passed by, slowing down to stare at us on the step. Molly flipped her the bird and the woman shot her own finger up in response.

"It's my hair," Molly said and I realized that of course the woman hadn't been staring at me; wearing jeans and a T-shirt, I probably looked like an average man. Tally ho and what a wonderful world we were in and all. But Molly would be the definite attraction this morning.

"Makes people think I'm a freak," she said.

"You could have at least combed it."

"Fuck that." She slurped the last of the eggs and put her plate on the step below her feet, but she did run a hand over the top to tame the more prickled bits of black and green down into the mess of bleached white. "She can think what she wants; she don't know what I've gone through the last week."

"Mm," I agreed. "I hear ya sister."

"You don't know either."

"You think I've had it easy?" I thought of the very easy bit of companionship I'd enjoyed just a few hours earlier, but even that had been tainted by the gender issue--was still tainted in fact, because it made my skin itchy, like it was too tight.

"You don't have it bad, Jay."

"As if you do."

She looked baldy at me. "Oh, I do. I've got it bad."

I mumbled a reluctant agreement and she protested.

"Okay, then," I said. "I'll bite. How bad?"

"Pretty bad." She looked at me and I could see the smudges under her eyes were still there despite the thirteen hours of sleep. The sallow look to her skin, the gaunt look to her cheeks, I'd already noted, believing that it spelled some kind of trouble even while I didn't want to think about what kind. So no, I wasn't that surprised about the baggie. Not really. Just angry. There was something else, though.

Something far more queer beneath her skin than her sexual preference. It sat on her and weighed her shoulders down.

"You said it was worse than just the drugs." I couldn't believe I was using the adjective 'just' to describe the blow.

She nodded. "Oh, yeah. Got me some shit brewing into a real stinky stew."

"You blowing a lot?"

"You saw the bag. It was full."

"Full of coke?" I couldn't believe it. There must have been a week's wages just in the corner of what was left.

"I got me a good connection in the city." She tapped the edge of the plate with her toe.

"Don't do that," I said.

She fell into contemplative silence after I spoke so that I regretted saying anything at all. I figured I'd have to wait her out, and was settled into the notion that I might have to prod her further, but within moments she was speaking again, all in a rush so that I had to watch her lips to make sure I was getting it all.

"Turned me a cute little ginger last weekend, you know, after you left; I walked around for 'bout half an hour but kinda lost my interest in anything. I hate it when we fight. Just hate it unless it's all in fun. I love you, you know. You get me. Don't know what I'd do without you. Maybe if we weren't such freaks we could--"

"Molly, get on with it."

"Huh?" She looked confused for a second, then abashed that she'd let herself get off topic. "Oh right. The ginger. Yeah."

"What about the ginger?"

"Underage."

It was a quick response, so quick and flip I doubted she was serious. I studied her face, trying to guess exactly what that meant. Underage could mean a whole lot of nasty for most people, but not for Molly. She had a way of wiping off shit as though it were honey.

Still, I needed to be clear about what was happening. "You turned her? You had sex?"

She nodded. "With a fifteen-year-old."

I should have been shocked to hear the actual number, knowing Molly was just a year younger than me, but my confusion about why this would be worse than a descent into stupefied dependant drug addiction clouded the reaction. "You mean that girl was fifteen? I don't believe it. She had to be at least twenty."

"That's what I thought--wait. You saw her? How--"

"Facebook."

"Right." She went silent, her mind obviously turning so quickly it had frozen her as she sat there. Then in a burst, she was up and running into the house. "I gotta get that shit off the net."

I followed along behind her, leaving the plates on the step, pushing the shoes out of the way that she'd tripped over in her haste to get down the hall. "It won't matter," I tried to say, but I doubt she heard me, so fast was she moving up the hall. She was in my bedroom by the time I'd got the door clicked shut.

"Seriously, Molly. It's too late."

She was clicking and swearing at my screen as I entered the bedroom. "Damn thing. You gotta get a faster machine."

"It's fast enough. Listen, Mol. You can delete it, but they keep that stuff on their servers."

"The Hell they do, what do they want with my pictures?" She'd navigated to her profile and was scrolling down through her wall, muttering curses at all the friends who had posted stuff. "Gotta shut this thing down. So much junk. Why do people have to tell me they're taking a dump? What the Hell do I care?'

"Molly?"

"Fuck. Farmville. I don't care if your crops are dying, you fucking prick." She shouted the last word, her frenzy growing to a pitch. "Damn fucking Monty, he's got nothing to do but play on Facebook all day. Farmville, Vampire fucking whatever, and Fishfuckingville. I don't give a fucking shit." She was getting shriller with each syllable.

"Molly." Getting her attention seemed as fruitful as a gay bar in the deepest South.

She clicked again and made a whooping sound. "Got it. Here, Jay. Here." She waved me over.

"Yeah, I Know, Mol. I saw it. Seriously, you can delete it but they'll keep it."

"Why?" She turned a dazed expression on me. Poor Molly so savvy in looking up porn on the net, so naïve in the repercussions of it.

I shrugged. "Maybe for stuff like this." I turned my gaze to the screen. The picture had been tagged by a dozen people. Molly had been tagged as Molly, of course; the couch was Aurora; the lamp, Dave. It looked like even the blurred baggie in the background had been tagged. I was stunned to see my name across it.

"There's some tag requests," she said. "Look."

I did look as she opened another tab to the photo requests. "Ha. They must think I'm dumb or something. I don't know those people. I bet she's trying to get me to open that pic up for proof.

"Don't accept."

"I'm not gonna accept. I'm gonna delete."

"But that picture doesn't prove anything, Molly." I said it, even though it did look pretty provocative. Still, I had a hard time believing the girl in the photo was fifteen. "You sure she's underage?"

"Quite a little looker huh?"

I studied the freckled face that looked back at me from the screen. "Not so much a looker, just kind of, well, mature looking." I didn't want to tell her I thought the girl was ugly.

"She sure knew how to--"

"Don't say it."

"I won't." Molly leaned back in the chair and crossed

her arms. "I'll just say I wasn't her first."

"I thought you said you turned her."

"I wasn't her first lover," Molly corrected. "She'd had sex before, that's for sure, but I was her first lesbian. She didn't know how to--"

"Don't say it. Really, Molly. I don't want to hear it."

She had the grace to blush. The bleach in her hair made great contrast for the boiled beet look of her face.

"So how'd it go down?"

She quirked her brow playfully, and I suspected my calm reaction to all this news had settled her back into a sense of normalcy. She'd want very badly to jump on the pun.

"You know what I mean," I said.

"Yeah, I know what you mean." She looked back at the screen. "She looked much older to me, too. Mind, I'd had a lot of coke by then."

I made a noncommittal sound but let her continue. "I met up with a couple gals in the bathroom doing crack. Man, they were fucked." She shook her head as though to clear the image.

I rolled my hands around in the air, trying to urge her to get on with it.

"I didn't take any," she said in protest, thinking obviously that I wanted to skip over the unsavory details of her drug use. In truth, I'd seen it enough, I didn't need her to paint me a picture. "Well, okay. I took some. Just a hit or two. Went back out to the bar. Never really found anyone I wanted to take home."

"I can't imagine," I drawled, remembering the getup she'd had on. The cravat.

"Oh please. I just had an off night."

"Could you get to the ginger," I said, losing patience.

"I am. You need to know the background."

"What background? You didn't find any crack except in the bathroom so then what?"

"So I went outside."

"Of course you did."

She nodded. "Right. You get it. There's always a few smokers outside, lurking about. Thought I could find a lady there."

"A whole bar and you could only find someone outside?" This was a first for Molly.

"Actually, no. No one out there would give me the time of day."

"Molly, really! Can we get on with it?"

"This is on with it." She stressed the verb with a whine, a sure sign she was losing patience with my impatience to have her finish. "You need to understand that I was pretty messed up by the time I met her."

"I don't need that background, Molly. I know you. You're a hedonist at best, but you're no child molester."

"Thank you," she said.

"Oh, you're quite welcome." I pushed at the chair so it rolled away from the desk and toward the bed. I sat down and yanked her to face me. I stared hard into her eyes, holding her chin with my fingers the way a mother would do with a naughty child. "I just want the nitty gritty, Molly. I don't need all the crap."

"Okay, okay." She put her hands up in surrender. "She was in a car out back. At least, I think she was in a car out back. I'd been out there for a while, you know, doing a few nefarious things with a couple of nefarious, criminal type fellas. Didn't want to waste the whole night, you understand."

I quirked a brow rather than speak. She didn't need further interruptions.

"There was an old clunker back yonder from a few better cars. She and another girl came from that a-ways. They seemed to know the guys. You know, got a couple hits. Made a few jokes. The ginger girl was like a gift from heaven, know what I mean?"

"Coincidence."

"No, no. Kismet. I'd been looking for just the right dish

all night. And bam. There she was. See what happens when you're patient, Jay?"

I didn't want to answer and ruin her train of thought. Instead I just nodded my head even though there were a hundred jokes in there about getting screwed ready to come out.

Unprovoked, she continued on, "I struck up conversation. Asked her about her job, her family. Shit like that. You know; you want to get laid, you have to seem interested."

"Never asked her age, though." Oh, the sarcasm in the tone.

"Why would I have to? It was way after midnight by that time. What good mother would let her underage daughter out and about at that time of night? Hanging around a bar? Hanging with those fellas? She had to be of age. Besides, she looked of age. You saw her."

"So the long and short of it is you took her home and screwed her?"

"The long and short, yeah."

I'd lost interest. This wasn't a big deal. Sure, the girl was underage, but how many teens gave up the ghost of their virginity even sooner. Sure, Molly was older. So what. A hundred men in a hundred and one would give away one of their nuts to lay a young girl.

"And so what's the problem? I mean, besides her age."

"Well, she wants money."

"Money?"

She nodded. "Lots of it. Says she'll report me for plying her with drugs--"

"Which you did."

"Which of course I did. You don't have a stash and not offer company some. It's gauche."

"I see."

"And she says she'll report me for violating a minor. She wants money, drugs, and money. In that order, or she'll report me."

I was beginning to understand. Extortion. Quite a different kettle of stinking fish. "That's quite a pickle."

"Indeed."

"So you've been out of your mind for a few days."

"Quite literally."

It wasn't like Molly to get this juiced up over something unless it really meant something serious. I had no doubt this girl wanted money and lots of it. I knew Molly was about as flush as an albino in a snowstorm. I also knew she had more drugs than money and more drugs than common sense.

I wasn't sure how I was supposed to react, or what I was supposed to do for her. One thing I did know, she wanted me to help her with the coke. And that was indeed something I could help her with. I got up from the bed where I'd been sitting, pushing the rolling chair back toward the computer desk.

"Where you going?" She said.

"To the kitchen."

There was a split second of silence, about all it took, I'm sure for her to figure out that I was headed for the baggie, with about a millisecond of reaction time added on. I heard the chair behind me roll backwards and hit into something solid--the foot of the bed, I presumed. Didn't matter. I kept walking.

"You can't, Jay. You can't."

"The Hell I can't."

She'd reached me by the time I got to the kitchen door and was pulling on my sleeve.

"Don't throw it out. Don't. Please."

I spun around. "Why show it to me, then. You were with me, were you not, when we dealt with Miss Thing from next door."

"Well, yeah, but--"

"But what?"

"But," she said, looking deflated. "I'm not ready." Even

her hair had fallen limp against her ears.

"Molly, you are ready. You wouldn't have come here if not." I realized something, then. "That's why you wanted to get rid of Stephanie. You were afraid she'd find your stash."

She pouted: a real one, not a feigned movement to charm me and I knew she felt sheepish. "Maybe we could keep it. Hide it. You know: for the ginger."

"You want me to stash this crap away so you can use it for your bribe?"

She nodded pathetically.

I said nothing. How could I? I mean, could you have found words to respond? Instead, I lunged for the baggie as though I thought she'd try to beat me to it. I held it up for her, upended it in the sink, and shook it. I saw her eyes close with a kind of panicked relief as I'd suspected they would. It was the addict in her that would fight; the Molly I knew would appreciate the freedom. Still, to be sure, I ran water from the tap over top.

"I think we need to get you some help."

She groaned. "Rehab."

I nodded. "You can keep Miss Thing company."

"What about the ginger?"

"I don't know. Really."

She chewed at the sides of her cheek. "I'll give you my cell phone."

It was all coming to me now. She wanted to duck and escape and leave me to handle her mess. I wondered if it was a fair price to pay to get her clean. "You're committed, right?"

"I'm tired." Is all she said, but the way the words came out, the way her shoulders had sloped downward with defeat, the smudge of shadows beneath her cheekbones, the jaundiced look to her skin: those all spoke of assurance in ways she couldn't have.

I'd been there before, you understand. Maybe I couldn't have noticed the weary sag to my own shoulders or the gauntness to my cheeks, but I remember the distinct sickness of an addict's own soul, that sense that I was better off dead than alive. But for me it was about more than it was for the typical addict; it was about that deep down sense that you didn't know who you were, that no one did. I thought of the countless times I'd stripped a razor blade against my skin, the times I'd medicated with drugs. I imagined Molly had never felt that way: raw, sore, and if she had, it had been so long ago that she'd forgotten it. Without thinking, my hand went to my side where those scars remained, a witness to my pain.

I heard her voice and looked up, realizing I'd blanked out completely, and that she'd been asking me a question.

"Huh?"

She stood with her arms crossed over, her gaze almost mean as she watched me. "You're not the only one."

"What?"

"You think you're so righteous because you've suffered. I've suffered."

I was confused. How could she have known what I was thinking. "I'm not self-righteous."

She made a mumming sound, like she didn't believe me. "You mutter to yourself when you're thinking." She inclined her head to where my palm still rested against my side. "I know how you got those," she said. "And that," she nodded toward my throat where the still visible long and silver line of an attempted suicide still reminded me of my will to live. "You forget. I didn't get this way overnight either," she said.

"Sucks."

"It sure does," she answered, and the way her own palm moved to cover her stomach, protective, like there was a fetus in there, made me think she had a few survival secrets of her own.

Some people had friends that they'd known since grade school. I'd only known Molly a few short years, but she was the best friend I'd ever had. Still, there were parts of her earlier life that I had no knowledge of. When we met, we moved forward. She was there for my suicide attempts, she was there for my drug induced medicinal states--enmeshed herself in them with me--she was there when I finally drove a stake in the demon addiction's heart. But that was all me. I always imagined I had more evil spirits than her; she always seemed so together. This was a strange turn of events for me, to think she had a few chasms in her spirit. I wondered for the first time what demons she'd wrestled to the ground and which ones still slept beneath her bed.

Chapter 15

We clambered out of a cab and entered detox together at 9:05 a.m. I had packed her a few of my femme clothes that would fit no matter the size of the wearer, but truth be told, since I was a bit more femme in girth than masculine, and since Molly was a bit hefty, we could wear close to the same size if we were careful about the cut and the material. Despite the C cups she sported and religiously strapped down, she had a very male physique. I threw in a few pairs of unworn and new panties: okay, thongs, if you must know, mostly just so she'd remember me every day and curse a little. I also found a few pairs of sweats that had *cutie pie* and *hot stuff* on the behind. She'd groan at those too, but I couldn't help myself and the sadistic nature of sending her to detox with such overtly girly things. For good measure, I threw in my feather boa and stuffed it beneath a pair of leggings so she'd find it later like a cockroach in her shoe.

There was also a longish dress made of sweatshirt material with big yellow circles on it. I hated the thing, but it matched Molly's demeanor that morning to a T. She was electric with anxiety, and I'd jammed the dress into her duffel bag before she could notice I was putting the uber-feminine thing in there.

The lady who checked her in gave her all sorts of instructions and to me only one: you cannot visit for at least a week. No problem there; I needed about that much time to decompress from all the goings-on of the last one. I wrote down the date on the back of an old receipt for mascara that I found in my purse, then snapped the sides together with a satisfying and final click.

Molly gave me a worried look; her hair was washed and smelled of lemons. She'd parted it on the side and flattened it out so it looked more everyday and very boyish. Devoid of the mask of garish makeup she usually sported with the freakish do, she looked puny and afraid. "But you'll come then, right?" she asked.

"Of course."

"Like, right first thing in the morning?"

"Like, right first thing in the morning."

The admin shot me a scowl, her perfectly bow-shaped mouth turning into a crooked line that made her pretty face look ugly. "You can't come first thing in the morning; they have group."

Molly gripped my arm at the word 'group'. "Jay?"

"It's okay, Molly," I said. "I will be here as soon as I'm allowed, and I'm sure 'group' will be just fine."

She seemed to have to work to find the muster for a grin, but eventually it came and it spread across her face slowly. "Some groups are okay." She waggled her eyebrows with a certain purpose that told me she was working at looking okay. The stud in the left brow caught the light as she wiggled it.

"It won't be that kind of group," I told her and passed her the photo I'd jammed in my pocket. It was out of its frame, folded in two so I could slip it in my jeans. I'd had my fingers next to it for most of the trip, touching it, making sure it was still with me. I had already memorized the slant of the baby's eyes, the fluff of black hair by her ears.

"If you see Stephanie, give her this. Something to remind her what she's working for."

Molly took it with a nod. "What about me?"

"Just think about me kicking your ass if you don't get better."

We said our goodbyes hastily since the nurse was all peppered with eagerness to get Molly in, settled, and on the path to righteousness Hallelujah. I threw a glance over my shoulder on the way out and noticed that although Molly seemed peaked and tired still, she was already touching the admin assist lightly on the elbow and letting herself be guided into the ward. She did have the decency to glance my way before she disappeared behind the two swinging doors, and the grin she gave me told me she would find the stay challenging in many more ways than either of us had anticipated. Perhaps that kind of distraction would be useful to her in her fight to clean up.

I crammed the cell phone she'd given me, into the side pocket of the purse I'd brought. Leave it on, she'd told me and charge it every other day. She expected the ginger to phone within a couple of days. "Probably by tonight," she'd told me with a trace of anxiety on her face. Indeed, tonight would be fine. I'd be ready for her.

The cabbie was still waiting for me, bless his heart and I thanked him with the agreed upon twenty dollar bill. When he asked me where I wanted to end up, it took me a few minutes to gather the courage to send him to my mother's. It was time to face the music.

"Think you could pick me back up in an hour?" I asked when he pulled into her driveway. Her Audi 8, a cool silver one, gleamed in the morning sun, but my father's Volkswagen Golf had already fled the scene. Off to work, I figured. His only solid excuse to part ways with my mother for a few hours.

I took the few steps to the front door and with a deep breath that sounded to my ears like a gasp, pushed it open.

"Mum?"

I waited a minute or so, almost praying there would be no reply. In the quiet of the hope, I stepped forward, shoes on, to work my way to the living room, dropping my purse on the telephone table as I went. I peeked around the edge of the door like a soldier coming home from Afghanistan.

"Mum?"

There was laundry everywhere, clean, because the

aroma of fabric softener invaded my sinuses. A shirt lay limp and long on the mantle, its sleeves dangling in the gape of the opening. A towel hung from the curtain rod, but threatened to let go its weak grapple on the metal pineapple filial. Various pieces of clothing were on the floor and couch. A pair of socks was tied together in what looked like an Asian nunchuck.

So they had been arguing, which meant Mum was somewhere in the house eating out of a quart of coffee ice cream that she kept in the freezer for just such an emergency.

I let out a holler that sounded exactly like her name. "Nancy." And was rewarded with the thundering steps of the guilty running to hide her shame. "Nancy, you get down here."

She called out in response, "Robert," she said, making me cringe at the use of my given name. "Robert, is that you?"

I waited beside the door jamb to the living room to give her the chance to hide the quart of ice cream as she came down the back steps to the kitchen. Sure enough, I heard the freezer door open and close. She came down the hall licking her lips. Her pleasure at seeing me standing there changed immediately to a look of guilty dismay that she'd been caught.

She stood off to the side of the door, an effect calculated, I knew, to diminish the effect of her smallness in relation to the opening. There was an almost gracile appearance to her frame, the bones weren't some meaty solid things thinning with age; they'd always been delicate looking. Her forearms reminded me of the lithe arms of a ballerina. Looking at her standing there, a tiny slip of woman in a purple housecoat and slippers, a person could be fooled into believing she was a fragile being needing protection.

The projection in her voice put me in mind of the Wizard of Oz.

"You've been fighting again."

So she'd taken in the leftover bruises and scar in under a minute; the guilt was slowing her down.

"I wouldn't say I was fighting. More like I was fought."

"You always seem to get someone angry at you."

I crossed my arms and hooked a foot over the other ankle. "Must be something about me."

She huffed. "You've got your father's mouth."

"I dare say it's more than that."

She looked me up and down and seemed to want to avoid that subject. She changed tack. "Took your time coming home." She smoothed her still long hair back where it had escaped the ponytail that lay plaited down the middle of her back. "I waited."

"I'm sure you did."

She looked down at my feet. "You left your shoes on."

She brushed past me to flick at a layer of dust on the telephone table. She examined her finger as though she had no idea how the dust had accumulated. Then shook her head frustrated.

I heeled one sneaker off then the other, flinging them with expert aim at the bottom of the coat tree like I'd done since the rack was put there in my early teens. I felt a trickle of sadism creep down my spine that led me to provoke her despite the way she was obviously feeling after her fight with Dad.

"I see you've been doing the laundry."

She waved a hand in the air dismissing the fact that the laundry was all over the room. "It never ends. Wash, dry, fold, put away. Wear, wash, dry, fold. It's like a plague."

"You can't know." She frowned at me. "What do you young people know? You throw-away generation. You wear something once and give it to the Salvation Army. I bet you don't even wash your underwear."

"You're right. I just give the dirty ones to the homeless."

"Don't be crude, Robert."

"It's J." I had no problem setting her button to argue, but the last thing I wanted to argue over was my name. Still, I would at least stand on that hill even if I had to die on it.

She ignored me, much to my relief. "Come. I've got a pot of tea on."

I followed her into the kitchen. "Milk?" she said.

"And sugar."

She tsked. "I didn't bring you up to take sugar in your tea."

"No," I agreed. "But I like it that way, I discovered."

She snapped on the kettle. "You seem to have discovered a lot of things since you left my care."

I stuck a licked finger in the air to show she had scored. "Nice," I said.

She turned as though she hadn't realized her counter provocation and put a delicate hand to her chest. "Robert, you think so low of me."

"J," I corrected again, and went to the fridge to get out the milk. I was beginning to regret my decision to come here. Surely I wasn't quite rested enough for this sparring that would have to go on before she felt as though she'd won at something.

"Dad get in your way again?"

"You know your father," she said. "He simply can't understand why I have so many things to do besides clean this humble abode of ours."

"Mmm," I said. "And I suppose he had the audacity to ask that you run a broom across the floor."

She cracked a grin, which surprised me. Her face lit up as it always did when she smiled, taking years off her face despite the wrinkling around her eyes. "I politely reminded him that I had far more important and soulful matters to attend to."

"The drama society?"

"Of course not. They are a bunch of low-lives living the masquerade of high society."

"I'm glad you realized that."

She dropped a bag into a two-cup teapot and tapped her foot as she waited for the water to come to steam.

"I dropped out of that dreadful play and decided to use that time to set up a soup kitchen for the homeless."

That dreadful play. I remembered our conversation about the argument she'd had with another actor. I guessed she'd been asked to leave and no doubt, she'd gone with a great feigned dignity until she'd come home to Dad.

"The homeless?" It was a staggering confession seeing as how the homeless in our rural town meant nothing more than Mommy's front door was locked after hours.

"Mum, there are no homeless."

"Well, you're just not looking," She lifted the kettle that had snapped to off and pouring a stream of water into the pot. "Your father said the same thing."

I looked around at the clutter of the kitchen: the potted plants that had died eons ago and had turned to dusty bits of crackled foliage, the microwave that had been left ajar and was filled with crumbs. There was nothing filthy about the house, rather a cluttered, abandoned feel. She loathed doing anything that resembled housewifery and had always found other things to do. Every now and then Dad would remind her that their prenuptial agreement of her being a housewife was that she actually looked after the house. He had, never since I'd known them been subtle, nor had he learned the art of discretion around what he said to her. He always blundered into conversation and lived to regret his choice of words. She always thought carefully before she spoke, which meant every word was calculated for some effect or purpose.

Like she'd said, I got a Molotov cocktail of both.

Still, knowing how it had probably played out didn't stop me from asking. "So what did you say to him?"

"I said nothing." She looked aghast at the thought I'd think she'd do something so low as to argue with her husband. "I merely rearranged a few things for him so he could better understand my situation."

Rearranged. It meant she'd thrown every piece of laundry at him one piece at a time. I could imagine the scene: her grabbing and wafting useless pieces of laundry at him, him ducking, maybe catching a few shirts. The pair of socks made sense, now that I thought about it. She'd obviously tied them together to give them some heft and launching power.

"Well, at least it was just laundry this time."

"Indeed. No turkeys or tin cans." She stirred her tea and pushed mine at me across the counter. It was in a leafy white cup and saucer while hers was housed in a delicate cottage China pattern.

"And your situation?" I stressed the last word.

She sipped delicately as she stood with saucer in hand and cup in the other. I noticed that there was some hardened coffee ice cream at the corner of her mouth that cracked as she made a moue.

"My situation," she said, *tinking* the cup to the saucer and moving to the table, "has nothing to do with the laundry. I know you think that, but it doesn't. They were merely what I had to hand." She patted the chair next to her and I obediently sloped over to take it. "I want to do some good," she said. "Finally do something worthwhile."

"So what's Dad's problem?" I couldn't imagine him, after all these years and indulgences that he offered her, that he'd take issue with her activities now.

"He has no problem, Robert," she said. "You should be ashamed thinking your father would give me grief over such an endeavor."

"J, Mom."

She scratched at the corner of her mouth where the ice cream was before reaching for a napkin from the holder in the middle of the table.

"He's a good man, your father. He'd never take issue with me helping others." She said this as though there was no interruption in her speaking. "No," she said. "He thinks it's the method that's inconvenient."

"The method?"

She nodded. "The soup kitchen. He says I'd have to first cook and that if I couldn't do it in my own house, then how was I going to do it for others?"

"Not to mention the so few others there'd be," I blurted.

"You sound just like your father."

"Mum, I didn't mean--"

"You never mean. You just blurt, like he does." She got up and put her cup in the sink. "Well, I plan to open it anyway."

"Mum," I tried to reason with her. "There must be another way to make a difference. There must be--"

"There's nothing, Robert." She threw her hands up. "What kind of legacy am I to leave? I'm 58- years old. Fifty-eight." She repeated the number as though it had crept up on her completely unawares and grabbed her cruelly by the nipple.

"I've got nothing to show for it. Your father has his work. He helps people all day. You're gone. You don't need me anymore."

"J, Mum."

"What?"

"J. My name is J, not Robert. Not anymore."

"There you go." She sucked her teeth impatiently. "See? You've got your little life and your so-called identities all figured out." She emphasized identities as though it made her stomach turn. I thought I felt my skin itch.

"My identities?" I wasn't aware she was well-versed enough in LGBT terminology to call it anything let alone a decent enough term that I knew what she was talking about.

"Yes. I read up on it. It's called Gender Identity Disorder." She aimed the sentence at me as though it were an arrow.

Well now, we were pulling out the terms, weren't we? Except I wasn't so sure, now, she had delved into the proper Internet places for the research. No self-respecting tranny would use that term. At least I wouldn't. Disorder. As though I wasn't right somehow. As though it was some sort of curable disease.

"Disorder?"

She nodded.

I jammed my hands in the front pocket of my jeans and realized the baby picture wasn't there anymore. I'd given it up to its owner.

"Mum, you have no idea."

"Oh, I do. Don't think I don't know what went on in that city."

"What went on was that I was running away." There the confession, finally.

But she didn't catch the confession or the sense of relief with which I delivered it, at having said it out loud so even I could hear it and know what it was. No. She heard only the words, not the sentiment.

"Running away from what? From us?" She shook her index finger back and forth in the air. "No. No. Not from us. You were running away from your disorder. You thought the city would fix you."

She was right in a way of course, just missing the critical elements.

"There is no fix, Mum. There's no fix because there's nothing wrong." I backed away, hands out and up, defending what little bit of myself remained that I thought I knew. I would remain calm, and I would not get upset. She was my mother. She meant well. She was depressed. I'd just leave and let this go.

She wouldn't let it go, however. She advanced, making me back up awkwardly until I was pressed into the corner of the cupboards by the door.

"They have therapy for that, you know. They let you talk. Give you some medicines to help you cope."

I laughed, scornfully. "Medicines? Do you know what you're saying?"

"I do. It's hormone therapy. They could give you testosterone."

"And then I'd be all better, right, Mum?"

"Well not right away. It takes time," she said, and then

continued, her voice a musing, quiet one, almost to herself. "I always wondered why you weren't very hairy for a man. Such pretty arms. Barely any beard." She put her hands on her hips, decided. "Makes sense, doesn't it?"

It's not my testosterone. You really don't get it."

I plucked at the T-shirt I was wearing, cursing already the thought that I'd left on such gender nonspecific clothing so she'd not see anything but what she wanted to see.

"This isn't me," I said, pulling the cloth away from my chest and slapping my thigh where the jeans were tight and coarse. "This isn't me. These are just clothes, Mum. They don't make me male or female. Hormones won't make me male or female. Nothing will make me male or female. I just am what I am."

There was a second, a flash, like a bulb flaring before it crackles out. It was almost there. I almost had it. I grappled for it, the word on my tongue, the definition of a familiar word, trying to send my mind to the back of the dirty closet, dig out the hatbox that stored the important papers. Shed some light.

But she spoke again, and the brightness was harsh and pointed like a shadow at dusk.

"Well, you have to be one or the other, Robert; you can't be both. It's unnatural."

I could barely hear my voice when I protested my lips were pursed so tightly. "It's J."

She stomped her foot. "I won't call you that." I could see her scanning the room, looking for something to lift and throw, I supposed, and my body went into full alert, cheated out of my moment of epiphany, and the anger crept up next to me like a shadow.

"Oh, no, Mum. You won't treat me like Dad. I won't take it. I won't just stand here and patiently let you wear out your frustration on launching missiles. I am J. You may not have named me that, but it's what I changed my name legally to."

I kept on, despite I could see she was on the verge of

tears. "Why can't I be both? Why? What's so wrong with recognizing both aspects of myself? What's so wrong with me admiring the feminine part of me that you put in there--?"

"You will not blame me for your problems--"

"Not problems, Mum. Fuck. I'm the best of both of you, can't you see that?"

"Not like that. You can't be both."

"I am both. You're missing the point. It's not like you can say to me, 'you can't have ice cream.' You can't tell me what gender I can be."

"I shouldn't have to tell you."

"Damn straight. I am what I am." My skin most definitely had begun to itch. I closed my eyes; I could so nearly feel the prick of a needle on my skin, the muddiness of letting go, that I could fly my spirit right out of here.

"I have a son," she said stubbornly. "I bore a son. I dressed you as my son. I sent you to hockey practice, I scoped out girls for you to date, I dreamt of grandchildren--"

I saw her swallow, her throat convulse as she tried to say more.

I took a step toward her. "Mum--"

She shook her head, threw her hands, palm facing me, in a defensive gesture. As though I'd hurt her. As though I could do harm to my own mother. As though I'd been doing harm so much, so often, and so long that she reacted instinctively, like a woman abused.

I rooted my soles to the linoleum. She placed a finger against the table as though to steady herself and I realized that it was more than her refusal to see me as bi-gendered, it was the ignorance of what that meant to her, to her little world of dreams. This legacy she spoke of was her fear of what my gender choice would mean to her. One more rite of passage I would rob her of.

"Mum," I said easing closer to put my arms around her shoulders. She didn't move. She could have been stone as she stood there and the itch beneath my skin scrabbled closer to the surface.

"What makes you think you won't have grandchildren?"

She spoke into my shoulder; her voice was in tatters even as she rigidly resisted me.

"How can I have them?" she asked. "You don't even know what you are." There was a sob beneath, one that I felt in the core of my own belly.

"How can I have a grandchild if you're a straight woman living in a man's body?" She shuddered. "How can you have a child with another man?"

I eased away, hoping she'd have softened, that the face I would see would show some resolve.

It didn't. Revulsion was written on her mouth, in the creases of her forehead. That she both loved and was repulsed by me was a shock. I'd never before thought I'd actually sicken her. She might as well have drawn a knife blade across my throat.

"I can't answer that for you," I said in all honesty. "Maybe I'll fall in love with a woman." It was a gesture made to stop a conversation I couldn't go on with, but I couldn't help thinking about Sherona.

She touched my chin, felt the cleft in it that we both knew was there. "But what would it call you?"

"What do you mean, what would it call me?"

"Mom or Dad. Would it call you Mom or Dad?"

She was pressing, urging me forward to a place I resisted. It's not like I ever wanted kids. I'd never truly thought about it before Stephanie and her baby. That poor baby failing to thrive despite obvious care, all the requisite things to keep a being alive: food, clothes, shelter. But something was missing. Something.

The scene with Sherona began playing in my mind. I felt her lips on my cock again, the gentle cupping of my testicles, felt again the softness of her palm on my skin. The weight of her breasts. I had to shake away the very real sense that at the time I could have cared less if she were a man or a woman.

I couldn't give her the answer she wanted, and I felt sick knowing what I'd have to say, knowing she'd weep when I left, that I would indeed hurt her again.

"I guess if I ever have kids, it can call me J."

She said nothing. I thought she was as emptied as I was.

"I have to go, Mum."

I left with a few minutes on the cab meter. He held out his watch to me as I got in and tapped the face. "You're cutting it close."

"To the bone," I said.

Chapter 16

I unlocked the door to my apartment and went straight to the kitchen for a drink. The empty baggie lay on the sideboard still and I crumpled it into a weak wad of plastic before binning it.

Water. I'd just have water. I picked up the titty mug and stared at it. Why the Hell not? I jammed open the cold tap and let it run for several seconds. Letting it get good and cold. Then I held the mug under the stream, like a blind person would, letting the finger slip in to test its fullness.

I roamed the apartment then, sipping from the mug, reveling in the feel of the fake boobs against my chin. I could enjoy it. Why the Hell not? I wasn't just some straight woman in a man's body. I was J. And J liked boobs.

I roamed into the living room, stopping at the sofa and picking at the Hudson's Bay blanket that lay puddled at one end. I pinned one edge to the other. I caught sight of my purse where I'd dumped it on the coffee table. I pulled the phone out and placed it on the table next to a tablet of paper. Only then did I realize the tablet hadn't been there before. It was one I usually kept on the kitchen counter next to the wall phone. I bent down. There was ink on it, scribblings in a beautiful, looping hand.

J. Phone me. S.

She'd spelled my name right. Oh, the joy of it. I could hear her speak the words, pronounce my name. The muddy sound of the way she made her syllables. I wanted to hear the voice again. I had a lovely pair of boots I'd get her to wear for me. A silken whip I'd get her to flail me with. I had a leather vest and cowboy hat I longed to wear again. I couldn't help the grin that stole my face as I picked up the phone and went rummaging for her number.

I swear I was going to press the numbers in when I heard a strange little keening sound. Like the mewling of a cat. Like the mewling of a tiny, newborn cat. I paused, finger hovering over the first seven in Sherona's number. Newly formed cat: kitten. Or if I knew Molly as I thought I knew Molly, another word for pussy.

Her phone was ringing.

I ran for it, lunging at the coffee table with a vehemence that shocked me. I had it all planned, what I would say, but somehow it had all left me. Shit. What was I going to say again?

"Hello?" Dumb, J. Dumb.

The voice on the other end was sultry alright. The ginger, no doubt. "I'm looking for Molly."

"This is Molly," I said, biting the bottom corner of my lip.

There was a pause on the other end and I held my breath. She'd surely recognize my voice was not the same tenor as Molly's. The question was would she question it.

The answer came with her question. "Do you have what we agreed on?"

"Of course."

"Then we should get together. I had fun the other night."

I wasn't sure what to say to that one; instead, I stayed quiet. Better to keep her thinking I was Molly than say more and have her know I wasn't.

She spoke again, obviously taking my silence for fear. "Why don't we meet at Tims? Out back."

Tim Hortons. Out back. That meant the large dirt parking lot where she'd obviously set up shop after hours.

"Time?"

"Half hour."

I choked. "Half an hour? But I don't have all the stuff." In truth, I didn't, but I didn't even know what the 'stuff' consisted of. Damn Molly and her bid to get clean, leaving me with this pile in my lap.

She laughed. "You wanna go to jail?"

I waited a decent moment then asked. "Ok. How much?"

"What does it matter?" she said, and I could almost hear her shrugging. "As much as you can muster of both."

It was then that I realized exactly what Molly was up against: no professional con-artist but a dime-store addict looking for quick money or quick blow or quick both. I supposed it didn't matter to a two-bit extortionist so long as they got some money and some drugs, they'd be happier than with nothing. It made it pretty clear to me that she really wasn't all that to be feared. She had no finesse. Two-bit indeed. I had no intentions of keeping the appointment. I almost laughed at the thought that she'd be waiting, that so-called fifteen-year-old twenty-something. We'd see if she was really underage.

I hung up and dropped the cell on the couch where if it rang again, it would be muffled. Then I went back to the kitchen to use my phone. I dialed in Sherona's number.

"Oh, thank God," she said when she realized it was me.

I smiled. "Maybe we could both call on this god together later." I felt all flirty and provocative.

Silence came from the other end and I had the horrific notion that she was going to break up with me. Break up with me? Hell, I guess I'd thought more of her than I realized.

"Sherona?"

"Yeah, J. Sorry. I'm here. Listen, I think we should talk."

Shit. You know what that means, don't you boys and girls and trannies. I heard the death knell across the phone. "We do?"

"Yeah. I just got off shift. Can I come over?"

I had a moment of panic. Come over?

"No," I said. "I can't do it here."

She sounded confused. "*It?* Do what, J?"

"Do whatever it is that you want to talk about." I was a coward. Shit, I hated being a coward.

"I said I think we need to talk; I didn't say we were going to do anything."

"But--"

"But what? I need to tell you something, and I can't tell you over the phone."

I pulled my dignity up over my ass. "Yes, you can. You can say it over the phone." It came out gritty. Nasty. I cringed when I heard my voice, but I couldn't help the fear that fueled it. "Say it. Just say it."

"J, Really."

"No *reallys* about it."

"J."

"J nothing. Say it, Sherona. Say it's over."

"That's not it, J. That's not--"

I swore at her. Something in my makeup, you know, that forces my mouth to become an ass under stress.

She was silent for a moment, weighing out, I supposed, how she was going to break the news to me. I waited with her, knowing what she'd say, hating that I knew it. I could hear her breathing--regular, rhythmic, then there was a sharp intake of air, as though she were about to jump into a pool of water.

"Say it," I prodded.

"I think you might have cancer."

I was a Leo, definitely not a Cancer. I wasn't a Libra. I wasn't a Scorpio, I wasn't a Goddamned White, Anglo-Saxon, bi-gendered fucking crossdresser and I wasn't a Cancer.

"I felt something," she said. "A lump. Some...ooze. On your left breast."

Breast? I had breasts?

I think I sat down. At least, my butt was on the floor. The phone cord could barely reach and I had to crane my neck up to reach the receiver. It was quite a stretch. When I looked at the cord, I could see that the spirals were nonexistent and that the thing looked so taut it could have snapped right in half. It was an old apartment; the owner hadn't thought to put in cordless. Stupid of him, really. On occasions like this, the phone could easily break. I didn't want that to happen. I'd surely get charged extra on the rent and here I was unemployed. I'd never be able to pay the extra when I could barely make it now.

I let go and for a second, I felt myself swinging like the receiver, back and forth, ahead and behind. It made circles while I watched it, while I felt my mind swim in time with it. A muddy female voice came and went with the pendulum: J? J, Fuck, say something.

Nothing. I said nothing. I mean really: what would you say when there was obviously so nothing to say.

She found me there after what seemed a day and a night. When she rattled my front door and stormed the apartment, I sought out sight of the microwave clock. Twenty minutes had gone by. Maybe more. Maybe less. But twenty was what I'd call it if I had to. I thought of those crime shows and testimonies on oaken stands. "And what time did you hear the gunshot Mr. McIvor?"

"J, it's J, Your Honor, and the gunshot came at twenty minutes ago." I crackled out laughter as I sat there.

"I'm sorry, J."

I looked up into the black eyes. I watched the plump lips move, made out some sort of sympathetic tone. "I'm really sorry. I didn't want to say that on the phone."

"I object," I blurted and cackled. Hell, but this was funny.

"Seriously, it was shitty of me."

"Leading the witness," I said.

"Leading the what? What the Hell are you on about?"

I made an effort to take her all in, to focus on her face, to assemble in my mind some sort of rational combination of hair and skin and lips. They were all blurry, as though I were looking down through a shallow pool of water at a beautiful fish. Nothing was distinct about her features. I settled on her clothes. She wore pink. I hated pink.

"I hate pink," I said.

She sighed and slipped onto the floor beside me. "I shouldn't have told you that. I mean, I'm no doctor."

"Oh really?" I looked askance at her. "Really, Sherona? You're not?" The edge of sarcasm was one I just couldn't help.

She picked at her nails. She'd been biting them. Whatever water had been blurring my vision now spilled down my cheeks. I wiped the wetness away.

"I'm so sorry, J."

I mumbled something, but it wasn't intelligible even to me.

"But I'm pretty sure you should go to the doctor."

"I don't have a doctor."

"Go to Emerg then."

"Why? Based on a lump you found? On me? On a man? On a man's breast? That's ridiculous."

"Why?"

"A man's breast, Sherona. A man's. A man doesn't get breast cancer."

She narrowed her almond gaze. "I thought you were a woman."

"Oh sure, bring that shitty stick up now."

"Well, what the fuck, J? What am I supposed to say?"

"Say fuck all. I do not have breast cancer. And you're not qualified to say I do."

"Have you noticed anything odd about your chest lately?"

I laughed. "This is fucking stupid."

"Have you? Have you noticed anything, milky, puckered? Anything?"

"Fuck you."

"You don't have to answer; just go to the doctor. Please."

"I told you, I don't have a doctor." I didn't. Really. I had a doctor's card from my stint with the bad boys of Yarmouth who had seen fit to re-introduce me to Yarmouth high society, but I had no doctor.

She sounded angry. "Then go to fucking Emerg, J. Just go. I'm probably wrong."

"Men don't get breast cancer. They don't."

"They do. It's rare, but they do. So go. Just go so I can be wrong." She got up then, and without a word, without a kind touch or a gentle caress, she left me sitting there. She just got up and left.

I let my palm run up my side, on the ribcage where I knew the scars were. I slipped my hand beneath the shirt and trembled my fingers up one, then the next and the next like steps to the Kingdom. Then I scrabbled them over, crablike to the other side. Tiptoed the tips up a few steps and over beneath my armpit. I pressed in. Circled around. I closed my eyes to focus better.

It was small. It was hard. It felt crinkled.

I caught my breath and refused to open my eyes.

At least I had an excuse now to tell Molly when I didn't make that appointment with her ginger.

Chapter 17

The cell phone rang for days as it lay on the sofa. The pussy ring. I made faces at it each time it mewled from the cushions. I counted the times it insisted I pick it up. The first time it rang, it rang twenty times. The next, twenty-one. The next, twenty-two. It was if the caller was on some psychotic math bender carefully incrementing one by one just to drive me to the brink of insanity. I had news for her: I was already laying sod down at the base.

The seventh time the phone rang, I let it go till twenty rings before I got up from the kitchen floor. If it was still ringing by the time I made it to the living room sofa, then so be it. I'd pick it up. No. If it was still ringing and it had made it to twenty-eight rings, I'd pick it up. Had to respect a person's intellectual persistence after all.

I got it at twenty-four. No use trying to push the envelope since I'd already decided to answer it.

The voice on the other end was shrill and very, very angry. No metaphor in the world could describe the vitriol that came through the tiny, mewling cell phone. "What the FUCK? You were supposed to meet me three hours ago. Three fucking hours. Where the Hell are you? You wanna go to jail? Do you really? Cause I can make it happen. I can."

"Are you sure it's been three hours," I asked. "My watch is slow. I thought I still had like, well, just a second here, I'll check my clock." I paused briefly for effect. "Oh, my, it's been...what time did you phone again?"

She spluttered on the other end and for the first time in three hours, in what felt like three days, I grinned.

"I don't mind running out now, if you don't mind me being early. Where was I supposed to meet you again? Your place?"

"Don't bother," she said. "You'll be meeting me in court."

"Listen," I said, and let my voice go to its full baritone, firm and stern. I channeled my mother in that instant, and knew without a doubt the young hoodlum would listen.

"I am not Molly. I am her friend. Her lawyer," I lied. "And I know you. I've heard about you." I ran through a list of things I'd done and said in order to get junk when I didn't have cash. I mentally ran my fingers through all those file cabinets and came up with:

"You scam for crack or coke or whatever you can lay your hands on, but we're onto you. It won't work this time. I don't know how many times it's worked in the past, but it won't work today."

"You don't know squat."

"I know twat, baby, and yours stinks to high heaven. Find another mark."

I hung up. There was a short bit of fluttering in my stomach that I'd done the wrong thing, but it was followed pretty closely by a sense of peace. She was, my intuition told me, a crackwhore. The worst kind: The most desperate kind.

The phone meowed again. I looked at it. It rang a second time. I picked up. You know me, I have a mouth. I like to use it.

"Hello?" As though I had no idea who could be on the other end.

"I'm sorry," said the ginger voice, this time velvet-smooth, and I was momentarily surprised.

"Sure," I said.

"Do you have anything to help a gal out?"

"You're joking."

Silence. I eased my eyelids closed. When threats don't work, try coddling. She must be desperate.

"Ginger?"

"Who?"

"You, you're a redhead, right?"

"Yeah."

"Well, Ginger, I suspect you need more than I can give you." I meant it. She needed more drugs than any dealer could handle, and she needed way more help than I could offer.

"You wouldn't know," she said, and while I expected the voice to be angry, even angrier than the initial contact, instead, it was soft, childlike. The vulnerability in it picked at the scab of my conscience.

"Oh, I know," I told her, steeling myself. Real or feigned, that vulnerability was the perfect bait for someone who didn't respond to aggression. I knew. I'd used the pity card myself. "You'll be doing this till you die if you don't get help. You know you will. Shitty life, I figure."

She hung up. I had to give it to her, though; she'd persisted longer than I would have. Maybe more desperate than I'd thought. I let my mind wander to what would happen to her now, to Molly. Not a teenager, the caller, not by a long shot. There'd been an aged cunning behind the calculation of her strikes. It was possible she'd been drugging for a few years, but I wouldn't have counted on her starting at eleven. Not here. Not in this town. She'd probably started at fifteen and in some sort of arrested development, kept telling marks she was that age when she thought she could use them for drugs.

I thought about phoning back and offering to take her to rehab. Could I make three for three? I had about as much chance of that as Satan had of sharing crumpets with the Almighty. But such was the stuff of drug use that I could feel the pity for her and want to help. Yes, even a stranger. I knew the stickiness of that particular lollipop all too well. It never left your psychic fingers no matter how hard you washed them.

I wasn't sure if she'd take to my advice, but one thing

was certain, she'd not be calling the police.

No use telling Molly that though. She could wait until she had the junk out of her system. And then she could wait a week or so more. And then she could wait a month.

She could wait till I felt like telling her.

I sighed. Please, God; if there is a God, don't let anything else happen. I was about as dry of wherewithal as limbo and my room suddenly felt as though it was as big and echoing as a football field. Little ole me standing in the middle, calling out to no one. I collapsed on the sofa and lay there, eyes closed, imagining all sorts of things clambering about the room so that I wouldn't feel so alone.

I wondered which angels, if they too existed, would be pressing against each other here, vying for their turn at me. Seraphim? Those vengeful arms of God ready to smite me for my past deeds, finally. Thus the cancer. Shit. The cancer.

I doubted Guardians. God no. I'd lost mine as surely as if I'd sent them packing lo these many years ago. Again: the cancer.

The cancer. I should phone Dr. Bashir. He at least was the one contact I had here in the medical arena. Well, now that Sherona had left me.

I felt an ache in my stomach at the thought of Sherona but it was just as well she was gone. Life with me would be far too complicated for a mere mortal woman. I'd need an angel. I opened my eyes, glanced around the room.

"Bring it on," I said to the emptiness.

I used Molly's cell to phone the good doctor. I didn't have the energy to make it back to the kitchen telephone. I wasn't sure if he'd answer or not as I remembered he didn't have a full practice. He did answer. On the second ring. How lucky was I today?

"Yes, I remember you," he said. "How's the ribs?"

Wow. He was good. "Healed nicely."

"The stitches come out yet?"

"Last one left to dissolve."

He waited for a moment then he said. "I have to get back to work. I'm in my office with a patient right now."

I understood I had little time. "I think I have cancer."

"Come this afternoon. You might have to wait, but I'll get to you."

He gave me directions, good detailed ones that I could pass on to the cab driver. Turned out I didn't need one. His office was within easy walking distance, right across from where the old liquor store had been before I'd left for the city. I waited in a pretty cushy chair for a doctor, pretending to read a magazine about gardening. Apparently, tomatoes were easy to grow on any back deck, and if you wanted to keep the lettuce you grew for longer, you just needed to wrap it in tinfoil. Well. I'd be damned.

I'd thought I'd be the only patient waiting, seeing as how he'd not officially set up practice yet. There was no office admin. He came and went from his inner sanctum with a shuffle of papers and folders, some threatening to spill out one edge. Not so, though. I was number seven out of eight sitting there and when an older lady came in, I got up so she could have my chair. By the time an hour had gone by, I was regretting losing the comfort of it. It took over two hours before the crowd had dwindled enough for me to be allowed a peek at his office.

He touched me on the cheek, feeling my jaw. "Healed nicely. I do nice work. No real scar."

"I've got lots of practice healing," I said.

"You think it's all about you?" He grinned.

"It has to be."

"Right you are. So." He settled back in his chair like an old world medic, seeming to have all the time in the world when I knew he still had three more patients out there and the threat of more any moment. "So," he said again. "You used the C-word."

"I have a friend who's a nurse."

"And this nurse says cancer."

I nodded.

"Well," he said, leaning forward. "That's why they're nurses. Not doctors. Let's have a look."

He aimed me to his examining room, a cold and sterile environment filled with noxious smells of chemicals and cleaners. I was a lab rat to be poked at, prodded, and examined. Lay back. Lift your shirt. No, take it clean off. How's this? This hurt? What about your testicles? Do you urinate okay?

I tried to steer the conversation around less clinical things. Maybe if I didn't speak of it, it wouldn't be true. "Why don't you have a secretary?"

"Not my style," he said, circling my left nipple with his fingers. Little pressure points moving in tiny circles. "You notice any discharge?"

I thought of the spots on my nightie that I'd thought was leftover Sterigel. I nodded stupidly, letting my mouth deflect the answer. "Not your style?"

"I'm setting up a sort of triage kind of office. Have a nurse take the BPs, the sugars, etc. before I see them. An admin can't do that." He moved to the right breast. Repeated the movements. Asked the same questions.

"But you have no nurse yet?"

He shook his head. "Haven't had a chance to advertise."

"I know one," I said.

"Oh, you do? The cancer nurse?" He pulled his hands away and passed me my shirt. "You can get dressed. Then come back out."

I took a minute to breathe then pulled on my shirt. He was sitting perched in his chair when I got back to his main office. He had his fingers steepled together. Not a good sign. You know how it is: steeple equals serious shit. Church metaphor and all.

"Well," he said. "I think your cancer nurse should come see me. She's a pretty good diagnostician."

"Oh God."

"Well, I'm not saying it's cancer for sure, but there's enough evidence to get some tests done. To send you to an oncologist."

"Fuck."

He pursed his lips: a pretty prim thing to do in light of what he'd just told me.

"Is it bad?"

He shrugged. "I don't want to get your hopes up, J. But I don't want to give you a death sentence either. I simply don't know. I'm more of a G.P. I imagine we'll get it biopsied and if it's malignant, you'll start treatments."

"It could be nothing."

"With men, this type of thing usually isn't nothing."

I tried to laugh. "Lucky thing I'm not a man."

He quirked a brow and I waved him off as though I was joking. "Nothing," I said. "I was just being stupid."

"You've been lethargic?"

"Well, yeah, but I thought it was because I was healing from the--well, from the beating."

"I should have noticed it then," he said.

I shrugged. "It could be nothing."

"It could," he said, but his lips didn't match his gaze. I knew he knew it was something.

"If I was a woman, I'd have been checking for this."

He nodded. "Sure, but at your age, you wouldn't have been frantic. Usually women in their forties, they worry. But hey, if it is cancer, at least we caught it."

"Yeah," I chuckled. "Like the AIDS. Catchy catchy shit."

"I'll book you for a biopsy and start looking for a good oncologist. Just to get the ball rolling. Hopefully we won't need one."

I said nothing. I took his appointment card that had the snakes and pestle on the front. Impressive. He'd already set up shop with fancy-assed business cards and everything. Didn't he realize he'd not need to go that far in a small town in dire need of medical care.

I left. I expected to feel something after the visit: dark humor, despair, anger. Something. I felt nothing. I walked out of his office and down the street in the sunshine of the afternoon as though it was any other day. I watched a woman in wedge heels and an A-line skirt leave the Old World Bakery carrying a coffee and some type of bread. She was having a normal day, no doubt. Out for a snack on her midday break.

A gaggle of schoolgirls in leggings and longish spaghetti-strapped tank tops stopped at the lights and waited for them to change. They chatted to each other with what seemed such ease; I felt a pang of envy. They all wore the same style, different colors, but distinctly the same. They'd not had a chance to exert their own fashion authority. Silly girls. I wondered if any of them dared step outside the box of teen fashion. A man walked with his Doberman on a leash, holding a baggie to the ready lest the beast feel the urgent need to defecate. Ha, I thought. Shitty, indeed. And there was the dark humor I knew so well. It hadn't gone AWOL as I'd thought, shocked into silence, but merely squatted in a corner till I gave it my full attention.

The humor's return was when I knew I was not going to be okay.

Chapter 18

I managed to phone Sherona and give her the details of the job. She tried to engage me in conversation. I had a headache, I told her. Just couldn't talk right then, but thought she'd appreciate the line on the job. She did, she said. She appreciated it very much. I was a Godsend. She'd go right down in the morning to drop off her resume.

There was a heated silence then, one I could feel burning into my chest. I wanted off the phone. I wanted to go into my closet, lie on the floor and stare at all the bras I wouldn't be wearing again. Then the ridiculousness of the thought made me chuckle into the receiver.

"What?"

I'd forgotten she was still on the line.

"Nothing. I have to go."

"J?"

My wrist began to hurt. I looked at it, white, strained. I realized my fingers clung to the receiver like it was the edge of a cliff. I forced them to relax.

She tried again. "J? I'm coming over."

"No," I said. "I really just want to lie down. Thank you for everything."

"You're not okay."

"No shit."

"You need someone."

"I need a good stiff slam," is what I said, "But I'll settle for a quiet nap."

I imagined she was remembering the feel of my old

wounds on her fingertips and lips, her tongue where she'd tasted the scar on my neck. She knew how they'd got there. She was undoubtedly imagining all sorts of endings to our little conversation: maybe all of them final.

"Don't worry, Sherona," I said. "I'm content to let the cancer get me."

I discovered my hand was laying the phone onto the cradle before I could come to a conscious decision to put it there.

I tried to go into my closet. I got as far as the doorframe. Really. You have to know I had every intention of going in there and saying goodbye to the girly things I owned. But I stopped just shy. I mean, I didn't have boobs anyhow, so why would I worry about not being able to wear a bra again? The clothes would fit me the same: I wouldn't have a mastectomy to worry about like a real woman. Like a real woman. That's what the trouble was. My body. My physics. My natal sex organs. The dichotomy of my gender and my being so separate, so distinct, opening like a chasm of shark's teeth.

To the max as the out-of-touch would say. Big Time. Holy Hannah and her huge hips and tits.

I wasn't a woman.

And I wasn't a man.

I ended up shoving on my shoes and heading to the bar. I ordered a ginger ale and a hot lobster sandwich from Renee at the counter and sat in a booth waiting for something to happen. Tense. My muscles set again to fight or flight. I thought of Stephanie's baby--that unseen, unknown little thing that hadn't made a choice about life. Just was.

I caught Renee's eye at one point and scurried my gaze back to the table. She came over anyway.

"Hey, J."

I nodded to her, then let my glance linger on the gouges on the wooden table, deep and inset with purpose. Three in parallel lines. Much like the ones on my ribcage. Self-inflicted. Bleeding the guilt out, the shame of all the things I wasn't. I shook away the image of my tongue lolling to the corner as I worked to make sure those lines on my skin were perfect in ways I could never be.

"You haven't touched your supper."

I pushed it away. She reached for it, holding it balanced in her hand, obviously waiting for me to say something.

"Not hungry," I said.

"You okay?"

I spared a quick look at her. She had on a see-through purple blouse with a lacy camisole. Her breasts peeked over the push-up bra beneath it all like two fattened mourning doves.

"Right as rain," I said.

"Sure, then." She hesitated a moment more then touched me on the shoulder.

I discovered I was biting my bottom lip and was relieved when she walked away, even though she kept glancing back at me over her shoulder.

A few patrons came in. The owner sat typing furiously into his laptop, making songs start and stop before they were even half in. I spared a thought to whether he was planning his nightly song list and then realized I didn't give a damn.

I stayed long after the sun god had pulled in his shingle for the night.

I'm not sure how many hours passed, but eventually I noticed a small puddle of youngish men hanging around the outside of the solarium.

I counted four; one of them kept peering around the corner as though he were checking out the back side of the place. I assumed there might be one or two more hanging about in the parking lot.

A drive beyond something I could name, bade me leave my seat in the booth and make my way out to the parking lot.

I hung close to the door for a few seconds, getting my bearings, making sure they planned to stay there for longer than it would take to mill over and introduce myself to the biggest and manliest there.

Yeah. I supposed he would do just fine. I noticed one of them pull a drag off a cigarette and hand it over to the next in the circle: weed. I almost laughed at how small potatoes it was. Almost. The gent being passed the joint was familiar in a gut-sickening way.

In fact, they all looked familiar.

I couldn't have picked a better crowd if I'd ordered it from the Sears catalogue. They might remember me. Then again, I could have been just one more victim on a Friday night that they'd beaten the freak out of.

It was entirely possible I'd have to remind them.

I sauntered over, hands in jeans pockets, lazy but purposeful.

"Share that shit?" I asked and directed my gaze to the original perpetrator. I looked at his feet. Yup. Those same Cat shoes. Please Lord, have mercy on this fashion sinner.

He looked me up and down with a narrowed gaze but passed the joint over. I took it, pinching my fingers tight, then held it to my lips and inhaled.

I didn't pass it back or pass it around even though it still had some burn to it. Instead, I dropped it to the pave and stuck my toe in it, ground it flat with a satisfying, oh so satisfying, bravado.

"Stuff is shit; just like I figured." I pointed my gaze directly at Monsieur le Cat Shoe, inclined my head. "'Course shit comes from assholes, doesn't it?"

A palpable tension hit the group. Nothing overt, you understand, just a mere shifting of weight from one foot to the other, bracing. Fists coming out of pockets, swallowing down of saliva. That sort of stuff. I'm sure you've experienced tension like that, and if you haven't, you'd recognize it. The air changes. Your cells make small talk with your body fluids in a way that dries up your mouth for the chattering. There's a beat: one...two...three in the sound barrier.

And the euphoria--dear sweet Heaven, the euphoria of

taking a certain path, of making your own prints on a trail less-traveled.

I think my ribs began to hurt right about then, even though no blow had been delivered. Cell memory is peculiar and it does so speak to the flesh.

It wasn't enough. It was never enough for my damned mouth. Where are you now, angels, where the Hell are you now?

I stepped closer to Cat Shoes.

"I'm thinking I'd like to take a manly man home, blow his brains out." I purred. "I'm thinking you'd like to be blown; am I right, you handsome scourge of other-minded people everywhere?" I reached out to touch his jaw line, an unpardonable sin worse than Satan's proud reach for the throne.

The angels were on wing, a choir of them, sounding in my ears, a frenzy of light in the dark. Or maybe it was just the electric feel of lightening touching my skin, melding my jaw into one large, very sore mass of crushed bone.

I thought I'd need to taunt him more. No need. Heavens, no. He was quite ready to beat the freak out of me. He was on me in seconds, and I was on the ground feeling the delicious pain of punishment so severe it was like a thunderstorm where light and sound come with no pause in between. I couldn't make more than a few guttural laughs anyway. No real language would form, despite my flesh crying out to my mouth to let go some words, some screams, some anything go. But my brain, oh my brain; it had its own agenda so separate from my body. It had chosen this beating. Not like before. Before it was helpless in its plight. Distanced, forcing itself not to feel.

Not this time. This time I allowed the beating. There was a difference, you understand. In the first instance, the pieces of me were scattered; this time they had come together.

I lay on the pave, letting him do whatever he wanted to me. If you must know, it wasn't that much different than a sexual trust that I put in him. I had to believe he was going to hurt me the way I had to believe a lover would not.

Freak, I kept saying to myself, echoing the words he hollered at me. Gayboy. Faggot. Oh, yes. Each thud of flesh on bone was punctuated by such lovely labels, they almost anesthetized the pain. Almost.

You know how the mind works. It finds ways to relieve pain if it must. My mind tried the only way it could: by sending me on fits of fancy and images of my past, my very bad past, that were acutely more painful than the physicality of the moment.

I saw myself in the bathroom at thirteen staring down at my penis and poking at it with a needle, at twenty jamming a different kind of needle into my arms, between my toes, the inside of my thigh. I masturbated in a church bathroom as a teen and an adult. I felt my seed exit and take every bit of soul with it. I felt cleansed each gaudy moment till just afterwards when that familiar black disgust came and drove me back to the needle once again.

I got flashes of silver too as the physical blows landed. Quicksilver, moving and fluid and mysterious. There was the silver of a razor slicing my skin, letting go the demons within if just for a short time. The sludge of heroin moving into a silver needle, the silver needle driving me back to the blade, this time on my throat, thinking: God, I can't do this anymore. I can't do this. Send me an angel, one God-forsaken, sexless angel to either take me or jam me back into this body with a core to care for and a reason for this, all of this, to be.

God. Give me something.

I was vaguely aware of a crowd thickening the group. I think I heard a woman's voice, and it sounded familiar even beneath the thundering within my ears.

"Shit, the cops are coming," that voice said.

Ginger?

They fell back, each one of them, and through bloodied and swollen eyes, I could make out a few shapes. The womanly face came close to mine. I took as deep a breath as I could. It cut through me like a blade. And then I felt hands on me, running down my arms, down my legs. Casing me, I realized. Looking for money.

"He ain't got nothing."

Cat shoes pulled her to her feet and I tried to talk. What I wanted to come out as, "Crack whore," actually came out as "more." I chuckled deep within, careful not to swallow the blood that had pooled in my mouth.

Still, she halted. I think she knew then. She heard something in my distorted voice that gave her pause. She leaned back down toward me.

"What'd you say?"

Cat shoes was cramming something into his pockets, making motions for his buddies to wrap it up.

"Leave him; he don't matter. You get anything?"

"Yeah, little bit," she told him. "From some stupid-assed hairy bastard out back." She sounded distracted. Her shoulders hung as though the weight of her hair had become too much.

The sounds of sirens came through the murk then and lights so bright as to burn the retinas. Ah, the Heavenly Host. Come, finally to do God's bidding. I'd be judged, now, surely. I didn't mind. I'd lived a horrible life, after all. The scuffle of shoes on pave as the choir grew larger, and of a car engine starting. A male voice hollering. Ginger was still a few feet away, waiting for the getaway vehicle to scoop her up, I guessed.

She looked at me again. Her voice was uncertain when it came, as though she believed she recognized me. I stared back.

"What are you looking at, fairy?" she said.

She'd mistaken the angels, obviously. Still, it took all I had to form any words, let alone anything intelligible. I did my best, you understand, and I'm not sure if I had hoped she'd be here or if I'd come trolling for trouble, but in that instant, with the choir still brandishing their swords ahead of me, pointing the way out with the light of their gaze, I forced my brain to force my tongue to say something that would matter.

God knew if I'd get to say anything ever again.

"Get help," I said, and I hoped she'd make out the words. I also hoped she'd understand that I didn't mean for me.

Chapter 19

I think Emerg was worse than the beating. I was poked and prodded in equally painful and humiliating ways and since I bored you with details of the beating, I'll spare you the pain of the inspection meant to repair that damage.

Broken ribs this time: four of them. Broken nose. Cracked jaw. Various cuts and bruises. Ruptured scrotum. I imagine you can taste the deliciousness of that heavenly joke.

The intern didn't see any humor at all in that one. She tut tutted over me, telling the policeman who hovered close, trying to get a statement, that I was in shock.

"You have to let me work," she told him.

"Get him stable," was the gruff answer.

I lifted a weak head a fraction off the exam table. "I'm a her," I said. "No, wait. I'm a him. Shit, maybe it's both. Hell. It could be neither." A froth of bubbled laughter choked off in my throat.

The doctor looked at me oddly as though she'd heard me speak, but couldn't make out the language. "You shouldn't try to talk. It's not worth it."

The RCMP officer inclined his head my way. "You make that out?"

She shook her head. "Too much swelling."

"He's in bad shape," he said.

"Her," I corrected again. "Her--I mean, *she*, is in bad shape." My head felt too heavy to even lay against the table. I wished it could fall right through the cushion beneath the sheet.

"I'll come back," the officer told her. "I can't make out a word he's saying anyway." He flipped his notebook closed and took three brisk steps toward me. "I'll come back later in the week. We'll have to hold them for a couple of days."

Hold them: the thugs. Someone must have born witness. I thought of the lights I'd seen. Maybe just car headlamps flooding the area with light, getting details and license plates. Not angels after all; probably just Renee. My eyes squeezed shut of their own volition.

I felt a needle jab my skin and almost protested. I was done with that junk, but then I didn't care and let my body relax. It would be a relief to be done with pain for a while.

I slipped in and out of sleep, mostly in, for a delirious amount of time. Nurses came and went, hooked me to things, unhooked me. Some of them prodded me awake and asked me stupid questions. I heard the constant blipping of my own heartbeat on the monitor. The tenderness of my body kept me from moving much, and so I felt the pins and needles sensation of body parts falling asleep and coming awake, much like my own bid for consciousness.

All in all, except for the interruptions, it was a restful experience. Uncomfortable, mind you, but restful. I didn't think. I didn't act. I just was. I suspected some of that had to do with the drip coming into my left arm. Morphine, I imagined. I hoped not. Maybe I should have told them I was an addict. At least there was a detox in the building. I'd just move from this bed to that one when I'd healed. Maybe Molly and Stephanie would still be there. We could be one cute little family up there, all frothing at the mouth and begging for junk.

By the next day, I think they started to wean me off the drip and they came at with me cups of orange liquid and bendy straws that they stuck in the corner of my mouth. A male nurse came round before dinner. He was a chatty thing. Talked to me and at me and around me, hustling about his round with a constant flood of words that seemed to press him into the room and then ebb against me.

"How are you feeling this morning," he said without waiting for an answer. "I bet you're much better than yesterday."

I hadn't known he'd seen me yesterday.

"You were pretty bad off, you know." His fingers went to my wrist, counting the heartbeats with the clip of his voice and checking it against the machine. "Good, good," he said.

"No, no," he protested as I tried to speak. "Don't bother. Your jaw is still pretty swollen. That'll go down in a few days, but it'll heal nicely they tell me."

He bustled to the other side of the bed. "I imagine the Mountie will be over today. He's phoned already. He says he has photos so you won't have to talk right away. They need something to hold those bastards longer."

Bastards. I was surprised he used the word in front of me. I gave him a good study. No mincing step. Handsome, manly features. Square jaw, flashing blue eyes, thick stubble. He was a perfect man.

He caught me looking and smiled. Then shrugged.

And I knew.

"Word is they kept calling you faggot," he said.

I couldn't say anything, and indeed, I didn't want to even be talking about this. It's not that the memory was painful; I just thought I'd gotten so far past that, that I didn't want to go there again.

He smoothed out the top sheet and tucked the blanket beneath a lip of white. "I asked for this shift."

He leaned in closer when he got close to my face so I could see his clearly. There was a sliver of crescent moon in the middle of one black eyebrow; he saw where my gaze traveled.

"When I was twelve. Same kind of ignorant bastards," he said and then mercifully let the tide of his words flush him from my room.

Indeed the policeman did come, maybe hours later, and indeed he did have pictures. My fingers hovered over the picture of the ginger, trying to decide what I should do. He helped me out there, and I wasn't sure if he was telling me her history because he wanted me to understand or if he recognized my hesitation. Either way, I was pretty sure he shouldn't say anything, but I was grateful he did.

"She begged to go to detox," he said, "but she's begged for that before. Last time she was caught trying to accuse some old man of raping her when she had broken into his house to steal his wallet. Two kids to support, so we let her go. It lasted about as long as it took for someone to pick her up in 24 hours. Those charges are still pending."

I let my gaze drop onto the face in the photo. Freckled. Bald looking, with an expression that appeared to be anger, but that I knew was something far deeper.

Her ginger hair was tangled into a ponytail, dregs of bangs swept to the side. My finger jabbed her in the cheek.

The officer grunted. "Good job. It's the best thing can happen to her," he said then he left, tucking his sheaf of pictures into a folder and beneath his arm. Maybe what I'd done in identifying her would help her. Or at least put her on the road to help. I knew she was trapped by her addictions; the same as those thugs were trapped by their own prejudices. Hell, we all were trapped by something.

I'm not sure how my parents found out I was in the hospital, but by the time they came, I was in a ward with another man recovering from surgery and was knocked out cold still from the anesthetic. It was a good excuse not to discuss the nitty gritties, as they--Mum, in particular--wouldn't want the others to know my--her-- nasty business. My jaw hurt, but the swelling, as the nurse had said, had started to go down. I could make a few intelligible words. I wanted to tell Mum I didn't need her there. I would be fine. They could go home and we'd put this behind us and never speak of it.

"Mum," was what I said, and I noticed both of them wore expressions I'd never seen before. I couldn't name it, but it made my face hurt. I realized with horror I was starting to cry.

She rushed at me and I was in her embrace, a gentle one that was both on me, but touching only the soft parts, the ones that didn't ache. How she found a few square inches on my body that didn't scream in pain was beyond me, but I leaned my forehead wearily against her bosom and felt my body heave with controlled tears. Thank God she was there. It would be okay now. It would be okay.

"My God, Robert," she said into my neck. "I thought that policeman was telling us you were dead. My God. My God."

Dad stepped closer and rested his palm on the top of my head. His voice, as always was far gruffer than a man his size should have been able to project. "We're so glad you're okay."

I nodded into Mom's chest. She shushed me, "It's okay, Robert, It's okay."

I knew it would be.

"J." I tried to tell her.

She chortled, misunderstanding my mangled pronunciation. "Yes, it's going to be okay."

She eased me back onto the bed, her palm sending shivers of calm across my forehead. "It's a good thing they have those ruffians in jail; they'd not live to do it again if I got my hands on them."

Dad shuffled over to a chair and pressed it into her knees so that she folded into it. He shot me a fleeting smile. "Your mother has already given the policeman orders. And I'm pretty sure none of them are legal."

"Messing with my boy," she said, disgusted.

Out of habit, I started to protest her use of the word boy and stopped short. What did it matter, really? To her, I'd always be her boy. It didn't have to mean anything more than child, blood of her blood and bone of her bone. What did any label matter, really? Just names. It's God's fault, really. You know it is. He told Adam: name these things and I'll give you dominion, a sort of power over another when you name it. The old South used the power of a word to hold the African population in their grips for generations until they took the word back and imbibed its power for themselves. The gay community had done the same with queer. I could do the same, I supposed.

They fussed about me for a short spell until Dad reminded Mum that I should get some rest. I nodded a thank you to him and closed my eyes. I felt her hover near me for long moments, fully expecting she'd give up and go home, but she stayed there and I fell asleep with her perfume in my nostrils.

I dreamt of Satan, strangely enough. He pulled kerchief after kerchief out of his ear, each one a different color, with a different word on it. I tried to read them, the words, and I had the distinct memory of eyeballing it closely like a nearsighted old man. The words mattered, you see. I needed to make them out. They eluded me, no matter how close I got.

The end of the line came with a set of wings that he grunted at when he noticed them flexing from his ear. One wing, then the next, opening slowly, ash-filled and spilling as the feathers shook open. He set them on his back and gave them a flicker to test the movement. I saw he had no genitals, and I realized it wasn't because he'd had the best parts of God but none, that he was able to extract himself from the Kingdom. He grinned at me and I woke with the feeling he was there in the room, lurking in the corner.

The shape huddled in the chair rose. It took me a few moments to come to consciousness enough to see that it was Sherona and that my parents had left. I tested my jaw with some relief.

"Hi,"

"Hi," she said. She had pulled the curtain around us, affording us some privacy against the man snoring in the bed next to me.

She was as beautiful as ever. The top she had on picked up flecks of green in her chocolate colored eyes. I wondered if she had an Anglo in her woodpile somewhere.

"I was worried."

I turned away from her to study the IV bag that had half emptied itself into my arm.

"I know you can't say much yet," she said and I felt her palm on my arm. "It's okay. I just needed to see you."

She waited, and I sensed it was because she was hoping I'd turn back to her.

"J?"

It was crisp, the sound of my name on her. She clipped the end of it, biting it off, making it a single letter. The way I liked it.

"J, I'm so sorry." She flipped her hand over so the top of it was against my skin. She ran that up and down my arm. The hairs tickled. "This is all my fault."

"Not," I mumbled.

I heard her shuffle, switching legs or something, maybe crossing and uncrossing them. I only realized she was moving around the bed when she stood in front of me again. She'd walked around rather than wait for me to look at her. She must have thought I was angry. I wasn't. I didn't know what I was, but it wasn't angry.

"I stopped on five at the end of my shift to see how Stephanie was." She leaned down and twisted so her face was close to mine. She'd had coffee; I could smell it on her.

"They said she's doing great. I saw Molly there too." She ran a finger along the length of my left brow. "I didn't know she was there."

I thought of Molly. She'd not have heard about my troubles, I didn't imagine, and I wouldn't want her to. I didn't want to ruin her recovery. Someone had to look after her, even if it was a beat up freak in a hospital bed.

"I didn't tell her you were here," Sherona said and made a move to pull the chair closer so she could sit facing me, tucked into the bed. She ran a light palm down my chest, inspecting; her eyes taking in each wince my body involuntarily made.

"She looked pretty happy. I thought she looked healthy, even. I guess I didn't realize how bad she must have looked that day. You knew, though."

I couldn't answer that. I did know. You can't suffer and not recognize it in another human being.

"Anyway," she said. "Stephanie's worker says she's doing really well. Has put on weight. Is talking about getting her baby back. She has a daughter?"

The daughter. The infant. I swallowed hard the lump that tried to rise. I nodded stupidly instead.

"I also heard she and Molly are quite the item in there." Sherona chuckled as though she were trying on the humor and wasn't sure how it should come out. "They try to discourage it, but they can't really prove anything either."

Molly. Insufferable. There was an ache for her that matched the dull pain everywhere in my body. It hurt when I breathed now, my groin was on fire. They must be weaning the painkillers down, the bastards, and I was finally able to feel each ache acutely. The pain told me I would survive.

"You?" I managed.

"Me? I'm fine."

I shook my head. "Why?"

She looked confused.

"Why me and you?"

Did she know what she was doing when she made love to me? Did she know we were crossing boundaries together? I couldn't form those questions; they were too much for me.

She touched my lips with her finger. "I like you."

I grunted.

"They beat you up," she said, "I hear because you came onto one of the guys."

I grunted again.

"I'm not sure what you'd call it," she said. "What you've been calling it. Transgender, bisexual, heterosexual, whatever," she said. "Doesn't matter to me. I like you because you are you. I made love to the person, not the body."

I grunted again and watched her watching me. I imagined she could see the thoughts flit across my face one by one and I let them play for her despite the gurgling of my soul that said they were a feast best left undigested. Oh, yes, I let them reel. The feeling of being on the fringe all the time, of feeling robbed of all the ritualistic milestones of growth, of being apart from humanity, that I sat outside the paradigm, excluded, and marginalized. I let play too, the feeling of shame that despite all that, despite the fact that the norm shunned me, I still wanted to be within it so, so badly.

So, what was I? Was I a woman in a man's body, a man in a man's body, a bi-gendered person in a uni-gendered body? A he, she, it? What, then? What?

And that's when I knew. I could eschew gender as quietly as it had crept on me, folding my cells into genitalia in utero, the same unconscionable way my DNA made my eyelids and fingers. The way my mother's body purged me when it was time, letting me gasp at the air and feed my heart that beat without her echo for the first time. Waiting for me to thrive without her.

Even Stephanie's newborn was smart enough at its core to understand that to thrive means more than to just exist. Even Satan must have understood it; he couldn't flourish where he was second hand to a greater being, and so, cast out from the world of heavenly host he'd known, he'd found a way to thrive. Surely he understood what he was doing. It wasn't about gender for him, oh no. It was about far, far more. He'd found a way to keep this little project of his creator's surviving but not thriving, robbing us of our joy by instilling fear, and with fear, the worry for self-preservation so strong we lash out in hatred and guilt and shame.

Oh yes. That angel-come-demi-god understood.

And now I do.

I'm more than the folds of skin that surround me, more than the gender that tricks me into believing I'm worthless in a world made of labels: be you woman or be you man or be you woman who looks like a man who wants to love a woman. I'm more than a mere mortal who suffers Satan's fall day after day.

Because I know what I am, what I'm meant to be, despite all my seeming humanness.

You can call me what you want.

I know I'm an angel.

The End